Migration:

Knowledge

by Walter Hopgood

Migration: Knowledge

First Edition, October 2019

ISBN: 978-0-9972147-8-9

Edited by Shavonne Clarke, found at
http://editsbyshavonne.com

Website: https://walterwrites.com – Twitter:
@walterwrites – Email:
walter@walterwrites.com

for Boo

Table of Contents

Prologue

Rhys turned and found Jason's bright, emerald-green eyes staring back at him, just as wide as his own. They stood transfixed, as if their shoes had grown roots and dug far deeper into the dirt than the spear that had just landed just between their feet. Rhys looked away for a second, focusing on the brightly colored pink fluff hanging off the spear's end. It had been placed there no doubt to help its owner locate it when thrown into wounded prey in the thick greens of the jungle. He looked back at Jason's pained expression; it was as if time had slowed down and they were treading molasses. The rich smell of dirt and grass hit his sinuses, the newly disturbed dirt and rocks that the spear had dug up spilling onto his boots. And while the smell of the mossy dirt might usually intrigue him, all he could do as he came out of his stupor was to open his mouth to scream.

But Captain Franks's bellow quickly

overtook his voice. "Run!"

The strong, meaty hands of Airman Luu pushed Rhys toward the Cludiant, the bulk of the massively built airman shielding Rhys from any further projectiles as Captain Franks yanked Jason out of his stupor. Each member of the group quickly returned to the moment, and before Rhys even realized it, he was running at breakneck speed in the noonday sun. He could see Jason out of the corner of his eye, and went to reach out when his husband tripped over his own feet. But before he could offer assistance, Captain Franks righted Jason as they approached the device. With his attention back on the well-worn pathway, he spotted the airman that Franks had left behind at the Cludiant as a "just in case." Except Airman Palomo's expression was anything but relaxed as the group descended on her.

As quickly as they'd approached, a glint of sunshine shone off the charm as Palomo pulled it from her pocket. She turned and dropped the charm into the slot, and half an instant later, the scenery of Terra flickered into existence, bringing along the familiar scent of ozone and a sense of relief to Rhys's frazzled brain.

Rhys tried to look behind him as he continued to speed for the device, his heart pounding in his ears.

"Nope," Luu yelled, urging him forward. So they pushed on as Palomo waved them toward the device.

He stopped only when a sharp pain bloomed in his calf, and looked down just in time to see dozens of rocks landing at his feet. Before his brain could make sense of it, more dirt arose from a newly landed spear, and he was lifted off his feet and manhandled through the Cludiant. An "Ow!" sounded behind him as he stepped firmly onto Terran soil before being pushed down by the airman.

The raised voices of confusion and urgency told him of his team's panic, though all he could see were dust and rocks as Luu's two-hundred-and-sixty pounds of muscle crushed him into the dirt.

Luu rolled off him and pulled him to the side, out of harm's way, which allowed Rhys to finally sit up. He turned around in time to watch the rest of the team hustle through, Jason flanked by Airman Thomas—one of the other airmen built almost as big as Airman Luu.

Franks's voice caught him off guard when she shouted, "Suppressive fire only!"

A hail of bullets quickly silenced the thudding of rocks following them from the alien world. And as Jason walked through the Cludiant, he ducked—even though those shooting were half a dozen feet behind him—and tripped over the base. He windmilled his arms and lost his balance between one beat and the next, and ended up on top of Rhys. Jason landed on Rhys's chest, pushing the air from his lungs so forcefully that Rhys saw stars for longer than what was probably safe. He finally focused just as the last of the airmen walked through, followed by Captain Franks, who reached down and pulled the charm from the other side of the Cludiant before walking through herself.

With no more gunfire to stop them, Rhys watched in horror as the very ticked-off people they'd just tried to meet rushed for the device.

Jason stood and pulled Rhys to his feet, and they moved out of the way of the device, just in case any of the maddening hordes of people made it through. He wasn't sure how many times the Cludiant had already pulsed, and felt Jason pull him even farther away as several rocks pelted the dirt at their feet.

"Come on!" he muttered as the device glowed one more time, the natives on the other side still charging. One got within a dozen feet, but just as the last pulse dimmed, the connection to the other planet disengaged, and they were once again safe.

As a first-time mission to meet people on other planets, the entire thing had been a bust.

Jason brushed himself off, his sweat-soaked brown hair plastered to his forehead as dust flew everywhere in Terra's windy, hot afternoon. "Well, what the hell was that all about?"

Franks turned to Jason in almost comedic slow motion. She shook her head, clipping Jason playfully over the ear—something she'd done a few times since getting to know the couple.

Rhys couldn't help but let out a breathless laugh at the familiar gesture as he pushed his own dark, much-too-long hair out of his eyes. "Offering them beef jerky? Really, Jason?" he asked his husband. He chuckled, running his hand over Jason's crazy mop of dusty hair.

"I was being friendly!" Jason's voice came breathy and playful. "I mean, who the hell knew they were even dangerous, with their foofy pink planet and all?" At Rhys's incredulous look, Jason added, "I mean, seriously! Their chieftain—or whatever he was, with the pink, foofy hair, and all that pink jewelry they draped on that cow-looking thing? How on Earth...

Sorry—how on *Terra* are you supposed to take people like that seriously? It looked like something out of a Saturday-morning cartoon."

"That cow-looking thing was a living representation of their gods, Jase," Rhys replied. "And then you went and pulled out and offered them beef jerky—"

"Hey, you know I get weird-ass cravings, boo," Jason said in defense, though a grin blazed across his face. He turned to Franks, who was smiling, even as she shook her head. "After we watched that fast food documentary, I made Rhys eat there like every day for a week."

Franks closed her eyes, then shook her head with a smile. "Back to camp, folks." She pointed to the collection of buildings a few dozen yards ahead. But *camp* probably wasn't the right word for their settlement anymore. Their small camp had grown from modest beginnings to a sprawling village, what with all the migration of people from Earth. "Well, I say we take that particular planet out of our rotation—at least for a little while."

Franks turned to the airman in charge of the charms, the triangle-shaped metal keys that fit into the Cludiant and somehow, through the combination of shape and markings, designated each one for a different planet. "Palomo, create a new 'beware of future visit' section in the collection of charms and store that one in it. Maybe we'll try in a few months."

Amidst Terra's blistering midday heat, it didn't take long for the group to reach their small village. With a nod to Franks, Rhys and Jason walked toward their cabin. Jason put his arm around Rhys, Rhys appreciating the small height difference between them as he slotted next to his husband, his hand resting at Jason's tapered waist. "So I guess this means I get to pick the next planet for exploring?" Rhys asked.

Jason just shook his head. "Damn pink planet full of hippie vegetarians," he muttered as he broke their embrace, then reached down to take Rhys's hand into his own.

Chapter One

Rhys and Jason's life changed drastically after the discovery of the Cludiant, a device that, along with the ever-present charm that had been handed down from grandparent to grandchild, connected Earth to a new planet. What had started as a tale in Jason's family about a device that could "take you to the stars" had gotten them kidnapped and nearly killed. The timing of the discovery couldn't have come at a better time, after crazed militants detonated nuclear bombs across Europe, forcing the migration of nearly a billion people to the rest of the world. Rhys's only complaint was that somehow, the new planet—a planet previously named Kepler 69d by the scientific community—had been nicknamed "Terra." Every time the name was brought up, be it in a report or newscast, Rhys complained that a little bit of his soul died. "Seriously, how the *hell* was a Kardashian allowed to name an entire *planet*?"

"You know what's really sad?" Jason had asked. When Rhys shook his head, Jason continued, "That you actually know what a Kardashian *is*."

Soon after news of the Cludiant's existence leaked, and plans to migrate part of Earth's population to the new planet had been floated as a possible solution to Earth's overcrowding, millions of voices spoke up, each ready to cross the galaxy and live on the new planet. Some simply wanted to escape what Earth had become after the destruction of wide swaths of Europe. While the continent had been mostly abandoned, other parts of the globe were way past capacity, with millions of new people straining local resources. While the leadership of Earth tried to bring back a sense of normality, some—from those in the media to random sidewalk doomsayers—managed to keep parts of the population vigilant to the point of over-exposed paranoia. Naysayers warned of a pending global apocalypse, now made even easier by populations crowded into smaller areas. The constant gloom and doom shouted by those naysayers had the effect of making Earth's agitated population want to flee, or at least consider it.

However, it wasn't the paranoid or scared populations who were the first to migrate to Terra. The first batch was a coalition of farmers as well as people of faith, the latter made up by several groups of Amish and Mennonites who knew how to live off the land without the need for much, if any, technology. Those who made the trip to Sacramento, where the Cludiant was still stored, were some of the most interesting; they were people searching for a simpler way of life more suitable to the 1800s, and had made their way on ships, airplanes, railroad, and buses to the California city.

Even still more interesting were the horse-drawn carriages that found their way down busy highways, often taking weeks to complete their journey. Entire families of Amish set forth across America. They showed up looking settled after their long journey, ready for a life on Terra. And more than one family had rejoined with their teenaged children, who had separated for a short Rumspringa. "My life is with my family," one hipsterish sixteen-year-old from Portland confessed in an interview before walking through the device with his family. He looked a bit out of place in such simple clothes, his multi-colored, dyed hair covered by a straw hat.

People often showed up at the base with whatever possessions they could carry—on horseback, pack mule, or just wearing a backpack of supplies. "It's like that guy from *Into the Wild*," Rhys had said to Jason as they watched a group of twenty-something-year-old men and women cross the event horizon, disappearing into the hot Terra afternoon.

The first few thousand migrants had taken off over the vast horizon of Terra, perhaps to claim their own part of the new planet. And with the planet being almost twice the size of Earth, with plenty of land, many ponds and streams for fresh water, and rich soil for planting, there was enough to go around for those wanting to settle. Rhys and Jason, along with Franks and several airmen, had done some initial surveys of the area, assisted by self-sufficient drones that mapped out the few-thousand square miles surrounding their initial camp. While they had the chance to move anywhere they wanted on the new planet, they chose to stay put in a small village that was quickly growing into a community because it was nearest the Cludiant. That made for easy and quick access to Earth when the need arose.

At first, travel back to Earth was almost every day. But as more time went on, Rhys realized that it had been more than ten days since their last trip back to their home planet. And that was only because Jason wanted to raid their personal stash of wine, kept safe in a storage unit back on base housing. "You know," Rhys said one night as he opened a bottle of pinot noir, "you could be this world's first winemaker, if you wanted."

Jason's eyes went wide with intrigue. But after a few seconds, he shook his head. "You know how long it's gonna take for grapes to be ready to harvest? And then we've got to make the wine, then age it." He shook his head. "Nope," he said as he took another sip. "But remind me to call Amber. Maybe she and her boyfriend will want to migrate out here and set up shop."

Rhys laughed. "As long as you get first pick of the vintage?"

Jason raised his glass. "I'll drink to that!"

Back on Earth, whole industries had started to rise out of the knowledge of the Cludiant and what it could do, which took many people by surprise. Replicas of the charms that had gotten Rhys and Jason off-world were manufactured and sold by the crateload, the hawkers extolling longer, happier lives for those who owned them. What was worse, however, were those promising quick processing and assured passage through the Cludiant to anyone willing to cough up enough money. It was all a lie, of course, since the military coordinated use of the device, but that didn't stop thousands of people around the globe from plunking down their life savings for a chance at a shiny new existence on Terra. But even those rip-off artists weren't as bad as those who made up advertising campaigns boasting of travel through the Cludiant like it was a luxury cruise.

"I guess some people will try to make a buck off anything," General Landingham told them as he handed over a glossy brochure during one of their visits. The military controlled the device, but people were inventive when it came to trying to profit in the still-fragile Earth economy.

Once they were settled into their new home—in something more akin to a double-size shipping container than not—Rhys tried not to think of what was going on with the Cludiant back on Earth. Instead, he thought of the infinite possibilities of discovery and exploration awaiting them. For Rhys, and for several other scientists who had come to Terra with them, the excitement of discovery was the real draw. Every time he and Jason had walked back from Earth to their new home on Terra, it seemed as if there was something else demanding his attention. The pulling sensation he felt as he stepped through the Cludiant never really changed, but each time they walked onto the soil of their new homeworld, it seemed as if there was a different bird call coming from the distance, or a new flower for Rhys to stop and study. Of course, new flowers led to Jason picking a few and bringing them back to their home. Rhys's scientific mind churned constantly on the new planet; Terra was an incredible world, filled with new experiences and endless wonder.

Terra, while unpopulated by any human-type life before the Cludiant connected the planet with Earth, had an abundance of both flora and fauna that provided the new residence with a ton of choices for foodstuffs, as well as plenty of raw materials that allowed settlers to build shelters and furniture to supplement the items from Earth. And while there weren't humans on Terra, there were plenty of fish in the lakes and deer-like creatures in the forests.

Soon after they'd migrated, Jason's parents, Mike and Donna, made the trek as well. Rhys knew that Mike was happy to find new adventures, but that Donna was probably ready to bury the memories of the European attack, and of Mike being lost in Europe for weeks before coming home to her. Only a few days after moving into their own shipping container-style home, Donna had settled in and was already being a mom to everyone around. "Now I can pester you boys until you decide to make me a grandma!" she'd said one night over dinner.

One of the first things Jason and Mike had done after settling was to take a few of the airmen out on a hunting expedition. Rhys had bowed out, queasy at the thought of taking down a live animal. But in the end, he was happy with the bounty they'd brought back. That night, under a spectacular double sunset, Rhys sat around a makeshift campfire with his family and many of the airmen to enjoy the fruit of their hunt. The creature had been comparable to an elk back on Earth, and had tasted nearly identical. "It really makes you wonder just how much our planets shared throughout history, doesn't it?" Jason asked around a mouthful of meat.

As more and more people made their way to Terra, the need for additional resources from Earth grew. But as the weeks went on, fields were tilled and crops were planted. While those crops would take a while, the food that the first settlers had was supplemented by Terra's abundance of fresh fruits, vegetables, and nuts. It wouldn't be long before Terra became self-sufficient, and might even be able to supply Earth with some of the resources they had stumbled upon.

In the grand scheme of the Migration project, self-sufficiency was the utmost imperative for the planet and her people's future.

Dependency on Earth was currently unavoidable, but the settlers hoped they could one day cut the cord, allowing them to be a truly remote colony. Just the thought intrigued Rhys, and plans for their new life often chased Rhys into sleep.

The only thing that bothered Rhys about Terra were the temperatures that followed them throughout the day. Climatologists had begun studying Terra and all she had to offer, and cited the dual overhead suns as the main reason for daytime temperatures rivaling Phoenix on a warm day. Scientists had also determined that Terra was in the throes of summer, and predicted much better temperatures once fall set in and the leaves started turning. Settlers escaped the heat at night, though it was still warm for Rhys, who had lived nearly his entire life in the Pacific Northwest. "I'm just not used to it being this warm," he said one night, sweat beading his brow. The fans surrounding their living spaces brought them respite from the heat, though nights on Terra could be comfortable.

Instead of responding, Jason got out of bed, clad in a pair of boxers and a t-shirt that clung to his defined chest with a light sheen of sweat. He held out his hand and walked Rhys outside.

"Where're we going?" Rhys asked.

Jason clasped their fingers together. "I think a nice little swim might be in order."

They walked along the path the engineers had cleared while a gentle breeze cooled their sweaty skin. Jason added a wink and squeezed Rhys's hand, his expression suggesting a little diversion in their future.

But as soon as they'd gotten to the pond, it was clear they weren't the only two escaping the heat. So instead of a romantic moonlit swim, they spent a couple hours with Jason's parents and about half the military contingency. And all was well until Rhys sneakily leaned in for a kiss, but as Jason closed his eyes, he pushed Jason off the dock and into the water. As soon as his head bobbed back up, Jason brushed the hair out of his eyes and swam to the ladder. "Oh, it's on, mister!" he warned, and then tumbled them both back into the cool water.

After their swim, they made their way back to the small village, where very few lights were still on. Sure, there were times when Rhys missed their neighborhood in Portland, but those thoughts were fleeting these days; now that they were settled in, Terra felt much more like home. The prefabricated house they came into—a step up from the tent that they'd called home for the first couple weeks on the planet—had everything they needed: a small kitchen, bedroom, bathroom, as well as a dining area that doubled as Rhys's office when the need arose. Rhys's parents occupied a similar unit just a few dozen feet away, along with others who had made the initial trip, as evidenced by the hundreds of small dwellings dotting the landscape surrounding their village. The military men and women on rotation from Earth were relegated to Quonset-hut-style barracks. But Franks, who had migrated to Terra alongside Rhys and Jason, had scored a small cabin of her own. She deserved it; not only was she in charge of Rhys and Jason's safety, she was also the ranking military personnel on the new colony.

After their aborted mission to the "pink planet," as it had come to be called, Rhys and Jason spent the rest of their warm afternoon at the military debriefing to discuss the mission, as well as come up with next steps. Franks brought up the list of charms they hadn't yet used. With little to go on, their first off-world trip had been a random selection. And Rhys hoped that the next one would be better. Hell, anything would be better than being chased by people with spears and slingshots.

They spent a couple hours in a warm conference room, figuring out logistics for their next trip. After, they made their way back to the small communal area where they'd cooked the elk. Mike and Donna sat in the shade, Mike carving a piece of wood and Donna reading a book. After a quick trip into their own cabin, Rhys and Jason went back outside and spent the rest of the afternoon sharing a cookout with

Jason's parents. There were laughs and memories shared until the dual suns got low on the horizon. Then, ever the romantic, Jason got Rhys to his feet, and the couple walked to a nearby outcropping of rocks to watch the suns set.

"I know sunset on the Oregon coast is beautiful," Jason whispered, as if trying not to break the moment, "but I could really get used to this." He pointed just as one sun set below the horizon, the other nearly there. As the sky darkened from pinks to oranges to dark blues and purples, the temperature dropped a few degrees, taking them from sweltering to just plain warm. And as night settled in around them, Jason stood up and took Rhys's hand into his own. They slowly made their way back to the village, exploring where they could.

After their latest walkabout, and as the two largest of Terra's moons shone brightly from above, they came home and each took a cool shower. Mostly dried off, but with a few drops of water sticking to his pale skin, Rhys sat bare-chested against their bed's soft headboard. He closed his eyes and let the cross-breezes of their ceiling fan and an old-fashioned box fan cool him off. His head was slightly fuzzy from the heat, but he needed to evaluate a new batch of drone images from the unsettled areas of Terra. He was deep in thought, making plans for an enormous solar array, when Jason sat down on the bed next to him, bare-chested, reading a trashy magazine he'd snagged during their last trip back to Earth. "What do you miss the most?" Rhys asked as he opened his eyes, making a notation on one of the drone images.

Jason waved the magazine in his hands. "This."

An easy chuckle escaped Rhys's chest. "You can't be serious." He looked away from the footage to the salacious article Jason was reading, the bold headline screaming, *The Guvernator's Secret Love Child!* "Of everything back on Earth, you miss that tripe?"

"Hey, sometimes you just have to keep up with Brad and Angelina's divorce, see what the Olsen twins are doing, and check on whether that crazy girl has been arrested again. And I didn't complain when you brought two hundred pounds of scientific journals across a galaxy, did I? Which I, delicate flower that I am, carried the entire way?"

"I believe"—Rhys bobbed his eyebrows suggestively—"that I paid that bill. *In full*," he added with a wink. The thought brought back the memory of that night, their first night out of the tent and in a real house, which Jason had insisted that they christen—nearby folks still in tents be damned.

"I don't know," Jason said, his words dripping with innuendo, "I'm sure I had to have done something recently to have at least earned me a tip."

Rhys couldn't help but lean over and kiss his husband. "You goof."

Before he could connect again for another kiss, Jason jumped up and stood next to the bed, then reached out and took Rhys's hand into his own. He urged his husband out of bed.

"What?" Rhys allowed himself to be pulled from the bed, even without knowing Jason's plans. He let the laptop slip from his lap, where it settled on the mattress, forgotten between one second and the next.

"It's too hot to sleep," Jason complained. "Let's go for a swim."

A second midnight swim in as many days? But at that moment, a swim in the cool, shallow pond sounded perfect. Rhys glanced at the clock at his bedside; it was late enough for it to be deserted. "You want me to get Franks? Your mom and dad?" Rhys asked as he followed Jason to the door. Even though it was a bit later than normal, he knew Mike and Donna's habits, and they were likely still up.

Jason stopped just short of the door and pushed his boxers down just enough for Rhys to glimpse the suggestive cleft of his husband's backside. "Not this time, boo."

Rhys followed Jason out into the night, grateful that there was enough moonlight to guide their way to the pond, but not enough to get them in trouble.

Chapter Two

One of the most interesting developments to come about after their migration to Terra was not only that they now had an abundance of planets to explore, but the technological marvel that the designers of the Cludiant had come up with eons before. The charms they'd found on Terra represented dozens of pathways between different worlds, based on the different shapes available. The method of how the Cludiant, along with these keys—or charms—actually worked to transport them across a galaxy was still a mystery, though scientists back on Earth were still researching exactly how everything worked.

But the most interesting aspect of the charms themselves was that they acted as a natural translator. Ironically, the discovery had unearthed itself back on Earth while Rhys and Jason were meeting with a delegation of dignitaries from around the globe. Jason was wearing his charm around his neck, and they were explaining the pulling sensation they had experienced while holding the charm near the Cludiant. They demonstrated the sensation by handing a duplicate of Terra's charm to the delegation. And as the charm fell into the hands of a woman from the French delegation, her exclamation of *"Sacré bleu!"* was met with a startled look from Jason. Rhys had been expecting a reaction from the woman—really, from each person who touched the charm—but he hadn't expected one from his husband.

Rhys heard his own voice go serious. "Sweetheart?" He put a hand on Jason's shoulder. "Are you okay?"

Jason ignored him, reaching out to touch the delegate, the start of a smile on his face. "What language am I speaking?"

The delegate looked at him, the charm still clasped tightly in her hands. *"Français."*

The smile on Jason's face grew huge. He turned to Rhys, unlatched the necklace, and put it in Rhys's hand, though he kept his hand tightly around Rhys's so that they were both touching the charm. He winked, then turned back to the delegate. "Can you please tell my husband that I think you've just helped us discover something new about these charms?"

"Moi?" was the delegate's response. But somehow the volume of her actual words were dampened, and the word "Me?" rang clearly throughout Rhys's brain, which caused him to start. She spoke again, but all Rhys heard in his mind was the English translation of, "This is amazing!"

"Wait." Rhys again turned his attention to Jason. "Why didn't we discover this on the first planet?"

Jason sighed, and they both thought back, though Jason was first to respond. "Oh, I was wearing it on the outside of my TAC vest." While Franks let Rhys and Jason call most of the shots, she did insist on each member of the team wearing safety gear. "I mean, I got a little bit of something that day, but I guess it wasn't close enough to my skin to register. And Palomo was back at the Cludiant, so she wasn't anywhere near the settlers."

Rhys considered it and nodded.

"Damn foofy planet," Jason said as they turned back to the delegation.

The French woman who had just helped them discover the translation capabilities cocked her head to the side. "Foofy?"

Rhys just shook his head. "This one's all you, Jase."

**

It was another week before Franks decided it was time to try another planet. While their hostile reception on the pink planet wasn't entirely Jason's fault, that didn't stop Rhys or Franks from teasing him. But it was Palomo, usually more reserved, who cracked everyone up when, at the end of the meeting, turned to Jason and held something out. "Beef jerky?" she asked, her eyes crinkled up at the sides.

Rhys couldn't help but mentally brace himself at the sound of the inserted charm locking into the Cludiant and the wisp of ozone wafting through the air. Like before, a serene scene painted itself between the beams. It was almost reverent, like a painting, for framed between the three beams were a multitude of colors painting the room on the other planet as if colored by stained glass.

After Franks gave the go-ahead, the team crossed through to the waiting planet and found themselves standing in a large room that seemed somehow familiar, the room mostly in muted, dark tones except for the light puddling along the floor.

Rhys adjusted his glasses as he glanced around; there *were* stained-glass windows that sparked sunlight along thick, dark stone walls, each window depicting people surrounding various other Cludiants. They must represent other worlds. As his eyes focused in the muted light, he turned to find the Cludiant they'd just walked through sitting along a back wall, with several rows of benches spanning the length of the room. And to the right of the device was what could only be described as a pulpit.

On this world, the Cludiant was clearly a religious symbol.

"It's like a church," one of the airmen said as she took pictures. And that was indeed what it reminded Rhys of: a simple church, but with ornate windows, each one telling a different tale.

"It wouldn't be unheard of," Doctor Sheila Burnaby replied. Sheila, along with Doctor Ingrid von Schoor, had jumped at the chance to migrate to Terra as soon as they were able, intending to study the device as well as join the exploration team. "Technology wasn't always demonized in the church—at least, not on Earth. Quite often it was revered by past cultures."

"Well this certainly reminds me of Saint Anthony's parish down in Newark," Doctor von Schoor chimed in. Though her voice was quiet, it still managed to echo off the walls. Footsteps accompanied von Schoor's voice, though from what Rhys could tell, the sound came from somewhere off the far walkway.

Franks gave everyone the signal to stop as the footsteps grew louder. With another signal from Franks, the airmen surrounded Rhys, Jason, and the scientists. Rhys was secretly happy that General Landingham had insisted that the team have a military escort for every off-world trip. Not that their first excursion to the pink planet wasn't enough reason. But when the footsteps were revealed to be coming from a portly gentleman who approached from somewhere deeper in the building, a smile on his face and hands up in supplication, the firepower seemed like overkill.

The man, dressed in a dark robe with a triangle hanging at his neck, cleared his throat as he approached the group, then touched the charm around his neck. He spoke, and while Rhys wasn't wearing a real charm and couldn't understand what the man was saying, he thought back to the French delegate, so he put his hand on Jason's arm. It was enough of a connection to the charm for Rhys to catch the word, "Welcome."

Jason—one of the few who had a charm—cleared his throat and held out his arms. He looked almost statesman-like. "We come in peace." He turned to Rhys with a wink. It was all Rhys could do to not laugh. After all, laughing at first contact with an alien world was probably frowned upon. Jason lowered his voice like he was about to share a secret. "I've always wanted to do that."

An idea crossed Rhys's mind, so he turned to Franks. "We need to find all the duplicate charms and assign one to teach team member," he said. "That way we're not caught off guard."

The robed man smiled at Rhys, then gestured to Jason, so Rhys clasped his husband's hand in his. Franks joined on the other side and took Jason's other hand. "Welcome to Messana," the man said. "Would it be helpful if you had more Illaminai?" The last word didn't translate, which he had obviously expected, because he ran his fingers over the charm hanging at his neck.

"Yes, please," Jason replied. "That would be most helpful."

"Come, come." The robed man gestured for the group to follow.

Hours later they sat amongst a group of Messanans, with Porwa, the gentlemen who had greeted them, introducing them to a dozen local elders. Initially, Porwa had shown them to a small room filled with thousands of charms. When Franks shone her flashlight, the shiny charms bounced the light back like disco balls. "We're not gonna put that in the report, are we?" Rhys asked as they each took a charm to help with the discussion.

"The number? Yes," Franks said. "But Jason singing 'Disco Inferno' and dancing until I turned off my flashlight?" They both turned to Jason, who had the biggest smile on his face. "I think we can leave that part out."

Jason smirked at her. "Poopy pants."

Once they were settled amongst Porwa and the elders who made up a large part of Messanan leadership, they began discussing the Cludiant. For the Messana, the Cludiant held a place of reverence, and though it allowed them to travel to thousands of worlds, they chose to stay on their homeworld, though they welcomed visitors. "Visitors," Porwa had said, "are like a gift from the Creators, just as much as the Illaminum is." It didn't take long for Rhys to understand that the words the charm around his neck couldn't translate were proper words for what the Messanans called the Cludiant, or the charms that connected planets.

"What can you tell us about the device?" Rhys asked during a lull in the conversation. "And the Creators—do you know who they were? And how they designed these devices and spread them throughout the galaxy?"

Porwa looked to those around him, then began to explain. "Ancients—who we know very little about, actually, except for what was handed down from generation to generation—found a naturally recurring element on a planet that had somehow been affected by the star they orbited, though it has long gone extinct. The material acts almost like a magnet, and the Creators saw in it the great gift it would provide. So their best and brightest scientists got together and came up with a way to infuse their technology with the material from this newly discovered planet and gifted us all with Illaminum spread throughout the galaxy, as well as Illaminai that could be used to connect a planet with others." He pulled at the charm hanging at his neck. "We do not understand the workings, but each planet has a specific 'charm,' as you call it. And you can connect two planets for travel as long as there is an Illaminum designated for the connection."

There was a flurry of conversation between the scientists and even a few of the airmen. "So how do often do you go off-world?" Franks asked.

Another religious man, dressed much

like Porwa, gave Franks a shocked look as he stood up. He was clearly scandalized. "After a trip to a planet that ended in near disaster for our elders, we have not set foot off Messana for many, many years. We welcome others, as long as they are peaceful and respect our wishes. But we have not traveled through the Illaminum since before any of our ancestors were born."

The explanation didn't sit quite well with Rhys. After all, scientific discovery was worth more than anything, even if it meant danger now and then. "By nature, our planet is full of adventurers. And even though there has been danger from time to time, discovery is what drives us." He sat up a little straighter, memories of the hot warehouse he and Jason had been taken to by the still unknown madman filling his thoughts. He tried to shake them off. "Drives *me*," he added. "If you have such a gift, why would you not use it?"

Murmurs filled the room until one of the elders spoke up. "Perhaps your experiences with the Illaminum will be different than ours. Each person is allowed to use the tools they have the way they wish." Emboldened by her response, the elder continued. "Why is your civilization, which looks so advanced with such weapons and technology, just now coming to use the Illaminum?"

Both Rhys and Jason gave Franks a furtive glance. Quick on her feet, Franks said, "Just the short version," to Rhys and Jason. So Rhys began the tale about their home planet, and how the device had been split up into three pieces and spread out across the globe for future generations to find. He told them about how the first beam was found by accident, and a sanitized version of their harrowing adventures that took them across the globe to find the last two pieces. And that the entire legend of the device was captured in a story handed down from generation to generation. He said that just by chance he and Jason were together, that it was his team that found the beam, but Jason's familial history kept the story of the Cludiant alive for nearly a thousand years.

Jason touched the charm at his neck. "My grandpa gave this to me when I was young, and started to tell me the stories that went with it. It's what helped us find the missing pieces of the device on our planet."

"That was just a few weeks ago," Rhys added. "We have since gone to only one other planet, though it did not go well."

Porwa nodded to the men and women surrounding him, and the elder woman who had asked the question eased a little in her seat, her expression smug. "Indeed," Porwa said, "which is why we do not go through the Illaminum anymore. Though we have been told of a planet that can probably answer any question about the device that you may have. I will have someone bring us the charm that connects our planet and theirs, and can help you locate one for yourself. They are a curious people, with more knowledge than can be kept in any library. They know everything, from the smallest creature that crawls underfoot—"

Jason gasped. The room suddenly went

quiet, all eyes falling on him. He smiled. "To the brightest star that crosses the night sky," he finished.

Several of the Messanans exchanged looks of wonder. Following a cacophony of voices, an elderly woman with deep wrinkles on her face leaned on her cane as she got closer and studied Jason. "How do you know of this?"

"Grandpa," Jason whispered. He suddenly looked a bit nervous, as all eyes were on him. "My grandfather." His voice came louder. "It was one of the stories my grandfather told me when he gave me this." His fingers touched the charm at his neck with reverence. "One of his stories is about the keepers of all knowledge." He closed his eyes for a second.

"Jase?" Rhys asked.

"Just a sec," Jason answered. "I'm trying to remember the way Grandpa described the key to me." After a few seconds, he muttered, "Animal, vegetable, mineral." He finally opened his eyes. "The key, at least for us, has an animal known as an elephant, a stalk of wheat, and three kinds of rocks. Grandpa said it symbolized everything known to man." He turned to Franks and waved to Palomo as he garnered their attention. "Does that sound familiar at all?" But each shook their heads.

After a bit of discussion, Porwa stood. "We shall endeavor to help you find what you need to visit the planet of knowledge. But until then, come, my new friends," he said as Rhys and Jason stood up. "It is not often that we receive visitors from other worlds. On Messana, you will be treated like royalty."

Jason laughed, which caused several strange looks. He gave Rhys and Franks a smirk. "First one of you to call me a queen gets it."

Franks and the few airmen in earshot chuckled as Rhys reached out and thwapped Jason on the shoulder before taking his hand.

Porwa led them to an elaborately decorated room not far from where the Messanans worshipped their Cludiant. Rhys and Jason took one side, and Franks the other, with the rest of their group filling out around the table. As they settled in, people flitted about, bringing in food and drink. "Porwa"—Rhys gestured to Jason, who handed him the necklace—"this is the symbol that connects the planet we came from, what we call Terra, to our home planet, Earth." He gestured to Palomo, who passed him the charm she had been holding. "And this one connects Terra with your planet." As he passed it back, he cocked his head to the side, then put his hand around Jason's arm as Jason locked the clasp of the necklace around his neck once again. "Is there any way we can identify the symbol that goes between Messana and Earth?"

The elder smiled. "That is for our scientists to decode and answer for us. Until then"—he paused as a platter overflowing with a roasted animal, surrounded by a multitude of vegetables, was set down in front of them—"we shall feast."

*
**

The trip to Messana gave Rhys and the scientists very little to go on in the way of technology or understanding how the device or charms worked. What it did give the team was the first planet they could come to with questions about the Cludiant, other planets, and perhaps trade. Rhys figured that there must be crops that Terra and Earth had, like coffee or corn, which could be quite valuable if they weren't found anywhere besides Earth. And as he sipped a bitter, warm brew that tasted more like sweetened, warmed mud with a mild heat than the coffee that he drank daily, he realized what one of their first exports could be. On their next trip, he would bring along a few pounds to share with Porwa and the Messanan leadership.

Overall, the trip to Messana was a success, no matter if they had been shortchanged in the way of answers about the Cludiant. But at least they came away with new friends and trading partners, which was worth something. And if they, perchance, were ever cut off from

Earth, they knew they would be welcomed back to Messana with open arms. That was always a valuable card to keep in their back pocket.

*
**

After a hearty meal, the team returned to Terra. Rhys couldn't help but smile as Jason and Franks traded barbs over being too full. "If all planetary meet-and-greets go like this," Franks said, "I'm gonna need to requisition new uniforms."

But besides full bellies, Rhys walked through the Cludiant with a few more charms—duplicates that the Messanans decided they could part with—and promises that, upon their return, pendants connecting Messana with both Earth and Terra would be theirs. They still didn't have enough for the full team, but they were getting closer. "I can go without," Palomo said as the charms were handed out. "I can't wear them, anyway. Something in them reacts with my skin; last one I wore gave me a rash."

"I can always share with Jason," Rhys said. "And we've always got the replacement the general gave Jason a while back." When Franks gave him a curious look, he added, "You know, for appearances."

Franks gave him a slow nod. "As long as we all have a way back home. Would do us no good to have this damn thing"—she touched the side of the Cludiant reverently—"if we got stuck on a planet without a way back home."

Chapter Three

Things had fallen into a comfortable rhythm for
the new settlers of Terra, and the number of
people migrating from Earth continued to grow
on a daily basis. But as time went on, and
project antagonists were given more prominence
in the media, the general feeling of unease about
the Cludiant began to mushroom on Earth. At
first there were just a few naysaying voices who
warned that the Earth was opening itself up to
alien invasion. That was laughed off, and the
benefits of the Cludiant were played up in the
media until a doomsday cult rivaling the size of
Jonestown left a very public suicide note as its
members staged a literal die-in in downtown
Toronto. The video was at the top of every news
channel for weeks. After that, the movement
against the Cludiant and migration project
seemed to gather support from all corners of the
Earth.

Unlikely alliances formed. A hardline biblical prophecy group denounced by most Christian organizations joined up with a separatist Native American group. The group raged from the shadows at first, but soon, members of the newly formed alliance against the Cludiant found their way from obscure corners of the media to the evening news, all the while demanding that the Cludiant be dismantled and destroyed. And while the voices were most often shouted down by those on the other side, the detractors' message was still amplified with scare tactics and used to send ripples of trouble throughout Earth's population.

Above all, General John Landingham kept abreast of everything going on that involved the Cludiant, no matter how inconsequential. His team, still led by Rhys, Jason, and Captain Tambra Franks, had had a difficult enough time when they scoured the globe to find the pieces. And they'd had an even harder time when they had the pieces but couldn't get the device to work. They had never caught the man responsible for kidnapping Rhys and Jason; the whole situation stuck in the general's throat like a bad seed. But beyond their kidnapper and his accomplice, Major Bartlett, just the very task of migration seemed almost impossible to manage, what with thousands of people showing up at the military base daily to make the trek to Terra. They had to be quarantined and screened to make sure they would not pose a threat to the device. Landingham had learned that the hard way, after a handful of the Cludiant's detractors had tried to get close enough to destroy it. If anything happened to the Cludiant, stranding hundreds of people on a foreign planet with no way of getting them home, the general would never forgive himself.

The connection between Earth and Terra was not continuously maintained because the scientists could not identify precisely how long the connection could be sustained—though it appeared to be infinite, based on the use the teams had been making. But beyond the device's unknown capabilities, there was a worry that overuse might unduly drain the Cludiant of its power. Again, another way to strand the settlers with no way of reaching home. Until there were firm answers to his and the scientists' questions, the Cludiant was used three times per day for six hours at a time, moving both people and data between worlds. While some looked at an intermittent connection as a bad thing, Landingham reminded the detractors that this allowed the teams on Terra to explore other worlds. To keep his team up to date, as well as keeping the people of Terra with computers updated as to Earth's news, data would be transmitted at the start and end of every connection. It worked relatively well, though it was a manual process. It was a pain, but the government put together yet another team, and he charged it to automate the process fully.

In true military fashion, regulations and processes were developed and put into place to keep the Cludiant—both the one on Earth, as well as the one on Terra—safe. And while guns and ammunition would be required items going to a strange, new planet, they and their owners were tracked throughout the process. There had been scuttlebutt from one of the Native American radical groups about blowing up the device, something that Landingham vowed would not happen on his watch.

But Landingham didn't worry solely about the people from Earth causing problems with the Cludiant. Now that they had a form of technology that could connect either Earth or Terra with countless other planets, even the craziest claims of alien invasion came with the hint of truth attached. And while they could control the connections between Earth and Terra with a schedule, they would be helpless if another planet could connect their Cludiant with Earth. He'd read the report from Franks about their latest contact with another world, and right now his team had a 50/50 record of peaceful dealings with other planets. Messana had garnered them some knowledge of the Cludiant, but the disastrous events on what Jason had called the "pink planet" had left him concerned, even if the incident was a case of "accidental expression of their gods being tasty snacks," as Franks had diplomatically put in her report. Before either of the off-world trips had commenced, however, Landingham directed his scientific teams to look for a way to make sure Earth and Terra stayed safe, and hoped for a way to block hostiles.

Landingham walked into the warehouse where the Cludiant had been staged and checked on how the latest migration was going. He felt happy that Sacramento was no longer in the throes of summer, though migrators to Terra were in for high temperatures. After checking, he walked into an air-conditioned office busy with scientists. "What have you got for me?" Landingham asked the group.

One of the new scientists, a short woman with spiky black hair named Farmington, shook her head as she handed Doctor McManus a sheet of paper. "Nothing yet, sir," she said as she turned to the general. "It looks like our best defense would be to remove one of the beams so that it breaks the seal, so to speak. That way the connection will be severed, even if the signal is jammed into staying open."

"Yes,"

Landingham cautiously replied, even   as questions swirled about his brain. "But can we do that without damaging the beam itself?"

McManus looked at Farmington, and both scientists shook their heads. McManus spoke up first. "The only way we will know for sure is if we try it during an active connection to Terra."

"And   risk   losing   our   outpost? Absolutely not." Landingham bristled at the thought, shaking his head. With as much money as was being thrown into the program, he had hoped that the scientists would be able to come up with something. But so far, the amount of knowable data they had about the Cludiant would fill a single page of paper, with plenty of room left over for the Sunday crossword.

Landingham turned back to the large

window and focused on the Cludiant, where a stream of people gathered on foot and horseback, some carrying all their belongings on their back, while others had horses and pack mules. The lucky ones had carts and carriages. It was like the recreation of an old west wagon trail, complete with the occasional swirls of dust. Landingham absently ran a finger over the nearest computer monitor and shook his head at the sheer amount of grime on the black plastic. He wiped his hands, then turned to the freckled, fresh-faced airman who watched the migration, capturing data as people passed. "How many are we up to, Airman?"

"488,325 with this batch, General," the young woman replied. "We're expecting to send through another sixteen hundred tonight. And at this rate, we should be at half a million by the weekend."

"Half a million?" Landingham nodded his head. He glanced at the young airman and gave her a nod. "Keep me apprised."

"Yes, General."

As Landingham headed back to his office, he considered the fact that so many people had already migrated to Terra. He himself was torn about the idea. He still had people under his command who now lived full time on the planet, as well as the team headed by Rhys and Jason. Two of his top scientists, Burnaby and von Schoor, had migrated as well, jumping at the chance to live off-world. And while Landingham was quite fond of Ingrid von Schoor, and she of him, he couldn't quite bring himself to take the plunge.

Landingham walked by another desk to pick up the latest list of intelligence data regarding threats to the project, like he'd done every morning since migration started. This time he scowled as he considered the thickness of the report. He knew he should read it as soon as possible, but at that moment, his heart just wasn't into it. Instead, it was with the memory of Ingrid the night before she left for Terra. She had urged him to come with her. "Maybe one day," he said as he walked out of the warehouse and into the mostly temperate autumnal day.

"Maybe."

Chapter Four

Rhys woke up to find an empty, cool space in the sheets next to him where the warmth of his snoozing husband should have been. He reached over and grabbed his glasses, then got up and wandered into the small kitchen where he found Jason, a mug of coffee in hand.

Jason bobbed his head toward the coffeemaker, something Rhys had declared was absolutely necessary if they were to leave Earth for a full-time residence on Terra. "There's still half a pot left."

Rhys walked up and leaned down for a kiss, Jason taking his attention away from the laptop for a split second before he went back to the screen. "Anything good?" Rhys poured himself a cup. He turned to Jason, and before he got a response, teased, "Unless you're looking up the latest tawdry Hollywood scandal." He ran a hand through Jason's bed-tussled hair, then took a seat opposite.

Jason shook his head. "Hey, I'm on the clock here." He turned the screen to his husband. "Looks like Franks got us authorization to head out again."

As he adjusted his glasses, Rhys squinted at the screen and read over the details. "Abundance, huh?" Abundance was the nickname they had given to the planet that had the most pendants in the jar they'd found; there had been eight of them. When plans came through to start going off-world, he had argued that Abundance would be their best option for a first planet to explore, because a plethora of charms had to have meant something. But he was overruled in that suggestion by General Landingham. It was easy for Rhys to defer to the general, having grown up with a militaristic father. Even easier when he considered that the military was running the project.

"Just a simple meet-and-greet." Jason stood up from the table. "Hopefully it's more like Messana and less like the pink, foofy one."

Rhys got up and went to the pantry, picking out a couple items for breakfast. "Well, this time I'm going to make sure you go through the Cludiant on a full stomach." He winked at Jason, who rolled his eyes in response.

"Oh, hey—I forgot." Jason hit a couple keys on the computer. "Leslie and Scott are migrating." He pointed to the email for Rhys to read. "She asked if we could be neighbors again."

Rhys looked out the small kitchen window to where Donna and Mike's prefabricated cottage sat a couple dozen feet away. "Yeah," Rhys said. "There's plenty of room." As Jason topped off his mug, Rhys added, "But how is she gonna get along out here without any rum?"

"Oh, you know Leslie." Jason laughed. "She'll bring plenty. And by the time she runs out, she'll have you and Scott working on a still for her."

Rhys couldn't help but bark out a laugh.

But in the back of his mind, he knew there was a hint of truth to what Jason was saying.

*
**

After a quick breakfast and a visit to Jason's parents to make sure they were getting on okay, Rhys and Jason met back at the courtyard in front of the Cludiant. The suns were high, though a few clouds had rolled in, which helped with the heat at what was, on Terra, supposed to be high noon. But because of Terra's size, that made it 2 P.M. local time. The planet was more massive than Earth, and as such had a longer, slower trip around its sun, Kepler, resulting in a 28-hour day. It took a little getting used to, especially when they had to keep appointments back on Earth. But the few weeks they spent on Terra reset their natural circadian rhythms to match the longer days that they experienced on the planet. It had all happened naturally, which pleased Rhys's scientific brain to no end. Jason said that he loved it only because it meant he got to sleep longer.

They stepped into a prefabbed hut that adjoined the Cludiant, their eyes taking a few seconds to adjust to the dimmed interior, even as light bled in through the windows. "Franks," Rhys said with a nod to the captain. "How's the migration going?"

Rhys sat down with Franks as Jason walked over to talk to the airmen. "And where are the others?" He looked around, not finding either von Schoor or Burnaby.

"They got called back by the general for something," Franks explained. "But they'll be back momentarily." She passed a piece of paper to Rhys. "We'll be crossing the half-million mark in the next couple days. And General Landingham says we'll actually ramp up soon after."

"Ramp up?" He tsked. "How much more can we ramp up with half a million people moved to an entirely new planet?"

"Well, with all these people we're going

to need more than just the basics. So the general has decided to set up a few clinics now that we have a better understanding of Terra's makeup, and some populations have stabilized in their new homes. Right now, the military is putting together a plan to build out some clinics to cover the basics, a couple per population segment. They'll stay until at least the Army Corps of Engineers comes up with plans for a few hospitals. Then'll come the schools and some community gathering places."

Rhys whistled as his mind boggled at how big the project had become since he and Jason strolled through the Cludiant carrying a tent and supplies just weeks before. Now they were planning cities with full-blown medical facilities, and that just made it even more real. He nodded as different thoughts about the migration competed for his attention, then shook his head to come back to the moment. After a deep breath, he asked, "So we're heading out to Abundance, huh?"

"Yep!" Franks stood. "You ready for

this?"

Rhys nodded. "I think, yeah. You know, as a human who's migrated from Earth, is standing on another planet, and is about to head across the galaxy to a third planet"—he gave Franks a sheepish look—"I guess I'm as ready as I'll ever be."

"Good." Franks called the airmen to attention just as von Schoor and Burnaby walked in. "Let's go make some new friends."

Chapter Five

As soon as Palomo inserted the key into the Cludiant and the distant landscape of Abundance came into view, Rhys knew this was going to be a much more important mission than the previous two. He didn't know why the thought had entered his mind, but it had. And he hoped that whatever they managed to find on the planet would be worth it. They needed another visit like the one they'd had with the Messanans, and it was all Rhys could do to keep positive thoughts in his head. He pushed worries aside and hoped that this one would go well, even as the niggling specter of doubt hung deep in the back of his thoughts.

While the Cludiant on the pink planet had been sitting unguarded and out in a field, and the one on Messana had been in what was essentially a church, the device on Abundance had been set in what looked like the middle of a market. They stood there in the morning sunshine, bright as any day on Terra but about thirty degrees cooler, which Rhys appreciated. Around them were tables, with foods neatly stacked and arranged in what looked like quite an efficient manner. And while there weren't any humanoids around, circular, possibly autonomous beings were restacking foodstuffs, transferring items between stalls, and tidying up even though the area appeared spotless. They didn't seem to have faces, though they each had appendages on either side of their round bodies that acted both as arms and steering, changing direction quickly and efficiently. The way the appendages wrapped around poles so they could turn, or picked up items to stack, the limbs appeared to be some cross between a monkey's tail and an elephant's trunk.

"Are these the people Porwa told us about, you think?" Jason asked. Though they had all passed through the Cludiant and stood just off the marketplace, their presence didn't seem to have attracted any attention. "These are the librarians?"

"Anything's possible," Franks replied.

Rhys just stood there, pushing his glasses up the bridge of his nose to study the beings working quickly and efficiently. Something about them didn't seem quite right to him, though he wasn't sure of what. "There's only one way to find out," he finally said, then took a couple steps forward.

One of the beings rolled up to Jason's side, using his calf to make a 90-degree turn around the group. But Jason reached out and grasped the end of the being's appendage. "Whoa, whoa," he said as the creature came to a stop in front of them. "Um, hello?"

A chirping sound came from a small hole he figured was a mouth, and it reached back out with what Rhys now considered more a tail than a hand. It gave Rhys a chance to study the beings up close. And while these beings seemed to roll everywhere, even on the broken pavement and cobblestones, now that he could see them up close he noticed that their skin looked fragile.

Almost transparent, in a way, and Rhys started to make out what seemed to be internal organs pressed against the surface of the skin, as if attached. He wanted to warn his husband to be careful. However, Jason didn't hesitate—he even ignored Rhys when he said, "Jase, wait," as he reached out and made contact with the being once again.

All was silent for several beats. Jason shook his head slightly, as if a chill had gone down his spine.

"Jason?" Rhys asked.

Jason finally let go of the being and turned to the group. "Well that was weird," he said as the creature rolled away to help others nearby.

"What?" Rhys and Franks asked in unison, while von Schoor grabbed a camera from her backpack and took pictures of their surroundings.

"They..." Jason began. "They don't exactly communicate." He gazed over at the beings. "I mean, they do. But it's so much more basic than anything else. What I got from…"—his voice trailed off once more—"*it,* I guess you'd say, was honestly just a series of pictures in my head."

"Pictures?" von Schoor asked.

Rhys didn't wait for a response. "Pictures of what?"

"Just basics, really," Jason said through a sigh. "It's like these beings don't have a structured language or anything. It basically asked me a series of questions—if I was hungry, thirsty, or needed shelter. When I responded no, it tried to let go, but I held on and imagined a large question mark in my mind. It quickly responded with the image of someone who had olive skin and looked more like us than them. And then it pulled away, so I let it go." Jason sighed again, shaking his head. "I can't guarantee this, but I got the feeling that it let someone know we were here and needed help."

"Why do you keep calling them 'it,' Jason?" Burnaby asked. "Did it not give you any type of indication it was male or female?" She stood a little straighter. "Or are they genderless? That would be interesting."

"I honestly didn't get any type of, well, *anything* specific from it," Jason said. "They seem to be some kind of amorphous blobs." He smiled, then winked at Rhys. "Kinda like me the first week after I found out about weed in college."

Rhys rolled his eyes, and as big as Jason's smile was, Franks's smirk was even bigger. Before the moment passed, Rhys took the chance to study the beings; they were about three foot high, their thin skin the color of a hazelnut shell. They had no distinguishing characteristics beyond the two long tails jutting out from each side. And while they were devoid of fur, many of them had what looked like scars scattered haphazardly around their body. Another one rolled by and stopped momentarily, which gave Rhys the chance to study it closer. The scars, lighter than the rest of the skin, looked more structured than accidental, though he was sure he didn't know how simple beings like these would be capable of caring for each other. Maybe they were helped by the planet's librarians, or at least the people that the creature had shown Jason.

"I know one thing," Franks said as they took in their surroundings. "I wouldn't mind these temps on Terra, that's for sure."

Now with the sun a little higher in the sky, the temperature had risen ever so slightly. But because of where they stood, a breeze pushed toward them, making their visit downright comfortable. "I mean, I like the midnight swims and all," Rhys said. Before he could continue, Jason caught his eye and bobbed his eyebrows up and down, looking like a Groucho Marx reject. "But I could get used to the lower temperatures here."

"Well, what's the plan, boss?" Jason asked.

Franks looked around, so they started scouting beyond the immediate area and found several low and mid-high buildings nearby. She began to point, but before she could get a word out, another of the beings rolled up to them. It offered its tail, thwapping at Franks's hand until she took it.

"Oh. Oh, yeah." She turned to Jason. "I know what you mean by symbols." The being started to move, so the group got out of its way and let it lead. "I think we're about to go and meet someone," Franks said.

The being made a clicking noise as they turned a corner and passed a much more tanned, slightly larger creature. Rhys felt bad; even though the beings were short and squat, they seemed to be able to move rather quickly. He was once again happy for the lower temperatures of this planet. If this had been Terra, they each would have been drenched in sweat by the time they were allowed to slow down. As it was, Burnaby looked a little unsure on her feet as she pulled at the baggy fatigues hanging loosely at her waist. Though you could tell who was military and who was civilian if you watched close enough, Landingham had decided that the team dressed as a united front gave a message of consistency, and made the scientists a lot less likely to be picked off.

After rounding countless corners, the being came to an abrupt halt, which caused everyone behind to nearly trip over the person they were following. "Are we there yet?" Jason asked.

"We need to wait here," Franks reported as the creature tugged from her hand and rolled away. "Whatever it said wasn't much, but the last thing that flashed in my head was the image of a sun crossing the sky." She turned to Rhys as she handed Burnaby a flask of water. "What do you think, Doctor? Think that's what it meant?"

As Rhys considered the imagery, it made sense. A sun crossing the sky was something that happened regularly, so that might be it. It was as good an answer as anything, he figured. He shrugged. "Sounds good to me." He looked around; though they were now off the central marketplace, they seemed to be surrounded by even more beings. "I just wish the sun wasn't in our eyes." He raised a hand to protect his eyes. The creature had dropped them in the middle of what looked like a courtyard. And while the area was bustling with activity, there was still not another humanoid in sight.

A warm and comforting feeling overtook his body. He turned in time to see a woman with flowing, dark hair and an olive complexion that reminded him of someone from the Middle East. If he didn't know for sure that he was hundreds of parsecs away from Earth, he could be fooled that this was just another ancient souq like those found up and down the Arabian peninsula, and the woman approaching in her colorful, flowing robes, a broad smile on her face, just another of the souq's many patrons. "There," Rhys said as he pointed to her.

The group turned toward the woman who had approached them, now with her hands outstretched. And though she didn't say a word, the overwhelming feeling she gave them was one of welcome and appreciation. Rhys couldn't explain it, and based on the looks that the others were giving her, he knew he wasn't the only one enamored by this stranger.

She came to a stop in front of them and smiled even more brightly. She made another gesture with her hands, nodded, and turned toward the entryway to a nearby building.

"I think we're supposed to follow." Rhys knew his teammates had heard him, though no one paid attention, even as they continued without question to follow the woman.

A few steps from the building entrance, the woman turned toward the group. It was like there was a list of rules being written in his head, though there was nothing in the rules—from keeping an open mind to being prepared to learn—that caused him to worry. An image of weapons and warfare appeared in his mind, and they were just as quickly painted over with a black X. He instantly understood the message of "no weapons" as easily as if their mysterious host had said it, and suddenly the three airmen were looking at Franks.

"Sir?" Airman Luu asked.

Franks looked around, then nodded. "Leave your weapons here."

The airmen quickly unstrapped their guns and left them on a low wall just outside the building. It took a few minutes, especially for Luu, who seemed to have not only handguns, but also knives hidden amongst his clothing. Rhys smiled when he remembered that it was Luu who had brought down one of the beasts on Terra back when Jason and his father had gone out as a hunting party.

"That it?" Franks looked at each person, then turned to Palomo. "Valentina?" she asked, giving the woman a smirk.

Palomo froze at first, then visibly relaxed as she sighed. "Yes, sir." She took a pistol from her TAC vest, then dropped two knives alongside it.

Franks shook her head fondly, but Rhys just stood there in awe. He wasn't sure how Palomo, who was not only the smallest in stature but the quietest of the bunch, packed away so many weapons. She was what Jason had nicknamed the "keymaster," as she was in charge of the charms whenever they went off-world. Apparently the nickname came from some bad 1980s movie that Rhys had never seen, where one person at a college frat party took everyone's keys so they couldn't drive. Somehow the moniker seemed to fit.

Still, so many weapons.

When the soldiers finished tucking away their weapons, Franks turned and nodded to Rhys and Jason. Rhys, in turn, turned to the woman who stood before them and smiled. He mimicked her earlier posture, holding out his hands from his sides as if to say they had nothing more to hide.

She gave them each a knowing glance before smiling and turning to the building. It had no doors, though whatever the structure was opened up before her. The only way Rhys could describe it would be walking from the stem into the bud of a flower as it opened in the morning sun. The vast, yawning entrance stood before them, and just beyond it, a brightly lit hallway.

Their guide turned and nodded, then gestured for them to follow.

It took some of them a second to find their footing, but Rhys wasn't hesitant at all. Any chance to learn was an opportunity to grow, a philosophy he'd learned early on in his career. Of course, back when he'd started, his friend Harvey had meant it more in the line of looking for new species of flatworms or moths while they were both helping a professor in the Everglades. But this? Traveling millions of miles across a galaxy? His opportunity to learn was so much more significant.

Though he'd barely spoken since meeting their host, Rhys had a hundred questions, each on the tip of his tongue, vying for his attention. He tried to bring some order to his thoughts, even with the cacophony of voices behind him that somehow begged for his attention as well. But just as he reached out to take Jason's hand into his own, a scuffle sounded from behind him. He turned just as the area was bathed in the bright oranges and whites of an explosion, and was almost knocked to his feet by the blast wave, his ears ringing as the blast echoed off every available surface. He tried to keep his eyes from rolling back in disorientation. After a shake of his head, he came back to the moment. And when he was finally able to focus, he saw Palomo splayed along the pavement, limbs akimbo, laying in a growing pool of blood.

He ran to the airman, passing Jason and the two scientists, who stood there in shock. He didn't know how he held it together when he found Palomo's leg separated from her body, resting several feet away. The only thing he could hear amongst the scuffle was Franks barking orders to the airmen. He looked down at Palomo's body, glad that those around him were quickly able to attend to the woman, who already looked pale from blood loss.

A thought flashed through his mind, and he considered the woman that they had been following. He turned to see if he could get her attention, only to find that she was standing just at the door's threshold. And around her were dozens of the circular creatures, though these somehow looked both lighter in color, and from what he could tell, free of scars. One of the beings grabbed another and pressed it up against the bloody stump of all that remained of Palomo's leg until the creature looked as if it were part of Palomo's body. Two other creatures picked up Palomo's severed leg and stuffed the end into yet another, then picked up the entire thing and started rolling off.

"Help us!" Rhys called as he looked at the woman. Her dark, uncaring eyes glanced over the scene like she was gazing at a painting and not watching a human being bleed to death. When she finally looked at him, she gave him the smallest of nods and raised her hands. And as she opened her mouth, those around Rhys fell, even as three more beings showed up and quickly rushed off with Palomo's body. Their host whispered something, though Rhys couldn't make it out. He opened his mouth to call out once more, but as she raised her hands higher and her voice grew louder, his vision started to go black. A feeling of comfort came over him, and as his vision faded, his body fell to the pavement.

Chapter Six

As Delia Bartlett propped her still-healing leg up on the footstool, she reached for the remote and upped the television's volume. "I'm starting to like this one," she said to the empty room. "All that fire and brimstone in such a small package." As the news presenter tried to get a word in, the feisty blonde on the screen continued to talk over her. Delia grabbed a couple more painkillers and took them, leaning back in the comfortable chair as the argument continued on screen. She looked down at the chyron and read the woman's name: Emily Bradley.

"The project should be shut down immediately," Bradley said. "It is an affront to our nature as a people, and the people of Earth. There is still so much we can be doing on this planet that we need to ask ourselves if just moving on to another planet is really what we want. How short-sighted is that?" The young blonde, smartly dressed in a crisp, gray suit, pushed a few strands of long hair behind an ear. "I'm not saying we need to abandon science, because science has gotten us so very far."

The host cut in, leaning into the camera as if to connect with the audience. "But if we abandon the project, what about the half-million people who have already migrated? Do we just leave them there? Shouldn't we do everything we can to learn about Terra? About our universe?"

The second guest, Chaske Oglala, a recent mainstay on debates when it came to all things Cludiant, interrupted Emily before she could resume. "What we're saying is, we have all these resources on Earth. And we have done a great number of injustices to our planet that we need to make right. We can't do that if we just send people off to corrupt and pollute an entirely new world. How is that right?" He looked directly into the camera. "We need to clean up our own home before we go and corrupt others."

The telephone rang, and Bartlett

scowled at it. She answered the call, but before she could say anything, the voice from the other side rang through with a solitary word: "Him."

Delia spent a moment contemplating the duo on the screen before turning back to the phone. "I think I agree," she finally said. "If we can bring him on board, we should be able to move forward with our plans." Though she couldn't see the man on the other side of the line, she knew he was probably watching the same program, perhaps with a scowl on his face. "Consider it done," she said. "In the morning, I'll see if we can arrange some time to meet with him and discuss a proper proposal." She turned her attention back to the interview and watched Oglala for a moment. "It doesn't seem like it would take much for him to see our side of the issue. Especially if properly motivated."

"Good," was the only word that came through the other end of the line. With a click, the line went dead.

Delia smiled and put down the phone. "Well now, Mister Oglala"—she pressed a button to summon her assistant—"let's see what we can do for each other, shall we?"

She sat back and watched until her assistant walked into the room. "That man." She pointed to the screen. "Find out where he's going to be tomorrow, get me there, and set up a meeting."

Her assistant nodded. "Yes, ma'am."

Chapter Seven

Rhys slowly became aware of his surroundings, though he didn't have to open his eyes to know that everything was off. While he could feel Jason's presence at his side, he knew they weren't asleep on their bed; whatever surface he was sleeping on was far too hard. The warmth he'd become used to since acclimating to the warm Terran mornings, cooled by the soft hum of the nearby fans, was also missing. And as he took a deep breath in, instead of the earthy, mossy smell he was used to, he got a nose-full of something a little more antiseptic. "Jase?" he asked lazily, reaching for his husband who snuffled quietly next to him.

As soon as he opened his eyes, all thoughts of mornings on Terra were ripped from his thoughts and quickly replaced by the horrors of this new, harsh reality. They had come to the librarian planet hours before, at least based on what he remembered. He looked at the custom watch that had been built on Earth, which kept track of the time and date on both Earth and Terra, an essential tool when they'd made the leap to living full time on Terra. From what he could tell, almost three hours had passed since they'd walked through the Cludiant.

Rhys shook Jason's shoulder. When Jason slowly blinked and finally came to, Rhys stood. He walked around the room and tried to rouse the rest of the team. He woke Franks first, then the two remaining airmen, Luu and Thomas. Once they were groggily getting to their feet, he reached von Schoor and Burnaby, sitting on their sides as they came to.

Airman Valentina Palomo was nowhere to be seen.

As everyone sat up and came back to themselves, Rhys went back to Jason's side to make sure he was okay. Once he was assured, he turned his attention back to Franks. "Palomo is missing."

It took Franks a second to come to her

senses. She looked around the small, sterile room. "She's probably scouting around. Maybe she woke up first and wasn't able to rouse us, so she went to look around the area." She turned to the two remaining airmen. "Luu, Thomas. You two spread out and see if you can find her."

"Find her?" Rhys asked, taken aback. "Captain Franks, Airman Palomo was injured. We all saw it."

"Saw what?" Jason asked. "Boo?"

Rhys looked around the room, not expecting the blank expressions on everyone's faces. They stared back at him as if he was losing his mind.

"I don't remember her being injured," Franks said. "Does anybody…"

The blank stares were all the reply Franks got. Satisfied that Palomo was safe somewhere, all eyes landed on Rhys. But instead of uncertainty, the group gave Rhys looks of concern. "Rhys? Are you sure you're okay?" Franks reached out and put a hand at his elbow, squeezing gently.

Rhys stood amongst the group, for the first time actually considering the thought: was he losing his mind? Had he injured himself when he passed out and imagined the whole thing? But as he closed his eyes, the horror of those few moments painted themselves on the backs of his eyelids. He could hear the explosion. He could smell the marketplace on the morning breeze, followed by the acrid scents of smoke and burned flesh. Then came the flashes of orange, and finally images of Palomo on the ground in a puddle of blood, her severed limb a few feet away.

It had to be real. It just had to.

Rhys opened his eyes as Jason put a hand on his shoulder, mentally bracing himself to re-tell his group what had happened. He wasn't one for violence, but he knew they needed to know the truth. But before he could start, the door to the small room swung open, and in walked a woman wearing a military uniform just like the other airmen.

"Captain Franks." The woman saluted.

"I've been looking through the building, but have yet to find any trace of anyone besides the beings we saw in the courtyard."

Franks turned to Rhys, a gentle smile on her face. "See, Rhys?" she said. "Palomo's right here, safe and sound."

He turned to the woman. She looked professional, yet a little smug. He studied her for a moment, taking in her olive-skinned complexion and long hair done up in a bun. He could feel all eyes on him, but he stood his ground as he shook his head. "I'm sorry, Captain Franks," he said, "but this is not Airman Palomo."

He took a step closer to the woman, and almost immediately Franks stepped between them. "Believe me, Tambra, I don't know who she is," he said as he studied her. "I take that back," he added as he turned to Franks. "She's the woman who greeted us after we left the marketplace."

He turned to Jason, who looked concerned. "You remember, Jason. Don't you?"

The room stood quiet for several seconds, so Rhys continued. "She met us just after we left the marketplace," he repeated. "Except she was wearing long, colorful robes."

"Then why is she wearing a uniform now?" Airman Thomas crossed disapproving arms over his chest. Even though both Thomas and Luu were taller than him, and each outweighed him by a good forty pounds of muscle, Rhys knew he wasn't in danger.

Still, he put his arms out, hoping to placate the man. "I don't get it," Rhys said. "But she's an imposter. She's not Valentina Palomo."

Franks studied Rhys so intently it made him uncomfortable. He reached back and took Jason's hand into his own. Jason always had a way of grounding him in uncomfortable situations, and he definitely needed at least a little bit of comfort, even if everyone thought he was crazy.

As quick as it'd started, Franks dropped her study of him and turned her attention to the woman who'd just entered and still stood at attention. "Name?"

Without hesitation, the woman responded, "Airman Valentina Palomo, sir."

"Parents?"

"Raoul and Estrella Palomo. Emigrated to the United States three years before I was born. New Jersey. Still live there, now with my grandmother, who emigrated just before her 70th birthday."

"What did your parents do?" When Palomo answered, Franks continued to question her. "What did your grandmother do for a living back in Spain?"

"Seamstress, ma'am."

"But what was her dream?"

"She…" The woman stopped, looked around the room, then turned on Rhys with laser focus. Her eyes narrowed a bit before returning to Franks. "I'm sorry, ma'am, but I don't know. My grandmother never told me."

Franks cocked her head to the side as she studied the woman. She took in a deep breath, then turned to Rhys and Jason.

"Ballerina," Jason said before Rhys could respond, and Rhys knew the answer was true. It wasn't something the usually quiet Palomo shared widely. It had slipped out one night at the dock while they were escaping the heat as the military passed around a bottle of Jason's wine. As they shared about their childhoods, from dreams to parents to the horrors they'd faced, Palomo had revealed that her parents had enrolled her in dance class with the hope of becoming a ballerina. It had been at the urging of her grandmother, who had dreamed of dancing her entire life, but "pirouetted like an angry doe," Palomo had shared in obvious mimicry of her elderly grandmother's voice.

Franks turned back to the woman in front of her. "Okay, so what's going on?" She took a step closer. "And where the hell is my soldier?" She glanced back at Rhys and gave him a slow blink by way of apology.

Rhys nodded his response.

"And who the hell is this?" von Schoor

asked. She and Burnaby had been so quiet that Rhys had almost forgotten they were there.

Instead of responding, the woman crossed her arms and again focused on Rhys. She took in a deep breath through her nose, exhaling as her expression softened. "Why didn't it work?" Her head cocked to the side.

While most of the group looked around, wondering what she meant, the woman remained unmoved, ignoring Luu's question of, "Why didn't *what* work?"

"What is it about you, Doctor Tambor, that prevented the process of what you would crudely call a 'mind wipe' from working? We've been doing it this way for hundreds of years now, and you're the first one it hasn't worked on."

"Never mind that," Rhys said. "Where is Airman Palomo? Did she survive?"

There was a collective gasp from several in the room. "Survive what?" Franks pulled Rhys's shoulder and searched his eyes. "What happened to her?" she asked, her tone thick with urgency.

"Oh yes, she survived," the woman finally responded. "We're just waiting for her to wake up, and we'll return her to you good as new." She smiled as she dropped her hands to her sides. "Better, actually."

Rhys took a deep breath and squeezed back when Jason's hand squeezed his, appreciating the callused skin against his own. He began to tell the tale of leaving the marketplace to follow this woman to the building where they now stood. And the explosion, the spattering of blood, and Palomo—their Palomo—who lay at the entryway in a puddle of blood, her leg detached at the hip, blown several feet away from her body. And then there were the dozens of round beings who surrounded them and carried Palomo off as the team lost consciousness.

"I will take you to her when she is awake," the woman replied. "Until then, would you follow me, please?"

"Wait, wait," Rhys said. The woman

stopped and turned around, looking at Rhys, a calm expression on her face. "Who are you?"

"My name is Esfani," she said. "I'm one of the many librarians here on the planet we call Comperian."

Chapter Eight

Rhys couldn't settle his gaze on just one thing, as countless volumes of knowledge tempted him at every turn. Esfani led the group out of the small room and down a brightly lit corridor lined with countless shelves and cubbies full of pictures, scrolls, books, and just about anything that could be related to learning. At least, that was what it looked like to Rhys. He took a moment to gaze at a scroll that looked fragile enough to crumble to dust if you even dared breathe on it. But temptation was too great, and when he tried to touch it, he realized it was bathed in some sort of protective energy barrier. Though he was inches away from it, the powerful field around the encasement had as much give as dried cement, though it was cool to the touch. It was abundantly clear that these people truly were far more technologically advanced than even the most cutting-edge technology on Earth.

"Esfani, huh?" Jason asked, quite out of the blue. "It's beautiful. Does it have a meaning?"

The librarian turned with a curious look. "It's a familial name. Though no, it holds no special meaning."

Jason shrugged, leaning toward Rhys. "You know, every planet we go to has people with exotic-sounding names. When are we going to find a planet where everyone's named 'Bob' or 'Mike?'"

As Jason bumped Rhys's shoulder, Esfani's eyes crinkled up at the corners as she laughed easily. "So where you're from, people are called that second name you mentioned?"

"Oh yeah," Jason replied. "My dad's name is Mike."

Esfani's smile grew, which caused both Rhys and Jason to look at each other. A few thoughts vied for Rhys's attention, and he finally asked, "So I take it Mike means something here on Comperian?"

Esfani's eyes dropped to the shiny floor and she forced the smile from her face. She leaned in close to Rhys and Jason. "In our language, that term basically means 'to have relations with a farm animal,'" which caused Rhys and Jason to both stumble-step, then bust out laughing. "But let's just keep that between us, shall we?"

They continued on, and Rhys knew that the blush on his face must be intense.

As he considered the technology and knowledge surrounding them, a thought popped into his head. "Wait a minute." Rhys moved past Franks to get closer to Esfani. "You spoke English. You're *speaking* English," he corrected. "In the past, we've had to use what we call the charms that come with the Cludiant as a kind of universal translator. How is it you're able to speak to us directly? And why now, when just before the explosion you were able to convey what you wanted with just a thought?"

"We are a very advanced civilization, Doctor Tambor," she responded. "We are capable of so very much. But at this moment, until we can judge the level of knowledge present on your homeworld, I cannot share with you everything we know." She smiled as they reached a doorway, opened it, and urged them inside. "At least not until you are ready."

Though the answer was satisfactory, it still didn't sit well with Rhys. He hated the fact that they were in one of the most prestigious learning spaces in the known universe, and yet the information that was to be offered to him might be limited. So much for learning at any cost.

"Before we start," Esfani said, "can I ask one question?" She looked around the table. "What prompted you to step through the device that first time? And why did you choose to come to this planet?"

When no one responded, Rhys offered his own answer. "A leap of faith, I guess," he said. "To explore a world beyond our own."

It was like Rhys had said the magic words. Esfani's expression warmed as a smile spread across her face, and she nodded. "Learning," she said. "Knowledge should be the ultimate goal of any maturing civilization."

Before Rhys could pepper Esfani with questions, Captain Franks leaned forward and put a hand on his arm, her expression cautious. Rhys understood immediately and nodded back, so Franks turned to Esfani. "So exactly why did you choose to render us unconscious? What happened to my soldier, and when will you take me to her?"

"Captain Franks," Esfani said as she gestured for everyone to sit around the table, "when your airman Valentina Palomo attempted to enter this, one of our most sacred buildings, she was carrying a weapon." She gestured to the center of the table, where the image of a grenade appeared. Rhys wasn't sure if it was real or not, but it was completely realistic, hanging a few inches off the dark, metallic surface of the table, bathed in light. "As I conveyed to you and your people before you were allowed entrance, there could be no weapons. So when your airman

Palomo tried to enter, our building's defenses kicked in, evaluated the threat, and took appropriate action. In this case, an uncontained explosion was called for."

"Uncontained?" Jason asked.

"Yes, Mister Frost-Tambor. We calculated that the explosion would not be large enough to damage our building, though there was an immediate threat to the airman herself. If the explosion were any larger, the airman would have been held by a field of energy and the explosion contained. Though if we would have done that, there would be precious little of the airman left to save." She leaned back. "Not that that wouldn't be possible."

Rhys was about to ask a question when Franks raised a hand up in his direction, though she never looked away from their host. "Doctor Tambor said that Airman Palomo had her leg ripped off, but you stated that you were going to bring her back 'good as new.' Are you so advanced that you can reattach severed limbs without any issue?" Before Esfani could reply, she added, "And what about blood?" She looked around the room. "We humans have very specific blood types. How would you be able to create human blood to transfuse into her?"

Esfani smiled, leaning forward and setting her chin on her hands. "You know the beings that you encountered at the marketplace? We call them the Illeuke. They have become invaluable to us here on Comperian. As such, we have come to rely on them for a great many things."

"You mean the round, kinda transparent things with two tails?" Jason asked.

"Yes, those," Esfani replied. "They are actually native to Comperian. We, as librarians, came here many, many eons ago. At first we lived with them side by side, without need for interaction. But now they are a part of everyday life. We could not do a great many things without the benefit of their existence."

Rhys looked at Jason, who held an expression of wonder. These were, indeed, a great people, capable of so much. "So what about the English?" Jason asked. "How is it you can speak to us—"

Rhys's mind was suddenly filled with Esfani's thoughts, even in her own voice. He looked up at her as she leaned back in the chair, her voice clear in his brain as she asked, "Would you prefer if we conversed like this?" She looked around the room, then continued assaulting his brain with, "This way we would be able to converse individually through our minds."

The room was eerily silent for far too long. Esfani finally broke the silence when she cleared her throat, then spoke aloud, "But I get the sense from some of you that mental communication is not quite something you are ready for." She looked smug.

"As for speaking English," she continued, "it was as simple as accessing your memories while you were unconscious. It didn't take long to put together a fundamental understanding of your language. Though I will say"—she looked over at Airman Thomas, who had a tendency to drop the occasional Creole expression, and then von Schoor—"some of you have a more, shall I say, colorful way of speaking. At least compared to the others."

Von Schoor barked out a nervous laugh, which caught on lightly around the table. "Oh, is it that I call my boss a jackass all the time?"

"Hey, that's some of the best flirtin' I've ever seen," Franks replied. "You know the general's sweet on you."

At the mention of General Landingham, von Schoor's face lit up, chased away by a quick blush. "That man, I swear."

"So," Rhys said as a means of getting back to the topic, "you can access our memories?" He considered Esfani for a moment as an Illeuke came into the room and brought clear bladders of what looked like water for everyone. "Is that how you learn about new cultures? You said that it was some sort of 'mind wipe?'"

"That's a very crude way of putting it," Esfani replied. "But yes, you could call it that.

It's a way to let us access your memories, as well as plant a few memories of our own. It allows us to interact with the people who come to the planet in an innocuous, close way. We remain within the confines of their own culture without contaminating them with our own. And when we have learned what we can, they are sent away, back to their own planet." She looked around the room. "What we are doing here in this room is somewhat unprecedented, and hasn't happened in a millennia. By the way, Doctor Tambor, we are still trying to figure out how you became immune to the process. Until we can figure that out, we have gone with the process our ancestors used ages and ages ago, which reveals much about ourselves to our guests."

Rhys knew that Esfani and her people had mental capabilities, but tried not to focus on it too much. He had been considering what was going on, but let the information stew in the back of his mind so as not to project it out for the population of Comperian to read. The charm hanging at his neck, while it matched the one that Jason wore which connected Earth and Terra, was the replica General Landingham had made ages ago back in Sacramento, before they had discovered the secret of the Cludiant. He wondered if Esfani and her people, having seen the pendant, assumed it was genuine. When no other solution came to mind, it was as good an idea as any other. Still, he tucked the idea back into the recesses of his mind. Even as he did, he knew it was something he should keep to himself—and not even tell Jason about it. Because whatever it was that prevented Esfani from accessing his memories, he wanted to keep it a secret as long as possible.

"Boo?" Jason snaked his hand under the table and grabbed Rhys's knee. He squeezed, and Rhys nodded his head.

"I'm okay." It wasn't exactly a lie, but all the same, Jason could tell that he was holding something back. Jason could read him better than any dozen people put together, and he hated keeping things from his husband, but the gentle cock of Jason's head and the way his eyes squeezed shut told him Jason knew he wasn't being totally forthcoming. But the situation seemed to call for it. "Ater-lay," Rhys said in a voice barely above a whisper.

"So what is this process of mind wipes and memory implantation, anyway?" Rhys cleared his throat as he looked around the room. But when he caught Esfani looking at him, she appeared confused. She didn't respond for several seconds, and continued to study him. As the silence stretched uncomfortably tight, Rhys finally asked, "What?"

"I've gone through the details of your language, but cannot come upon a reference for what you just said. 'Ater-lay?'" she asked. "What is that?"

Rhys kept a straight face, but Jason barked out a laugh that quickly reverberated around the room. "It's just—" Jason started, but Rhys cleared his throat as he knocked Jason's knee with his own under the table.

"It's just something that Jason and I say

to each other sometimes." Rhys turned and winked at Jason. It was odd that people with such advanced knowledge and technology would be stumped by Pig Latin, something he hadn't used since probably elementary school. Still, the less they explained, and the less he and Jason used it, the better their chances of keeping secrets if the need arose.

Satisfied, Esfani sat back in her chair. She glanced up, and it was then that Rhys and the rest of his team did as well—and that was when he realized the source of his unease. The group was seated in a room like an old-fashioned operating theater, where medical students would sit around and watch an operation. Except the people seated in the gallery above them sat quiet, dressed in the same lightly colored robes that Esfani had been in, and watched the situation intently.

Franks pointed to the gallery above. "Who are they?"

"As I said," Esfani replied, "we have not done this type of work in hundreds of years. As such, elders who we have all studied under, as well as new librarians, have decided to watch the process." She got up and walked around the room much like a university lecturer. "Here on Comperian, our primary purpose is to learn all that we can. Not only learn, but document that knowledge so it is available for future generations." She gestured to the side, where picture after picture painted itself against the stark, white wall, each image lasting only a second before dissolving into the next. In each image was a book, a scroll, stacks of papers, and even some paintings that looked hieroglyphic in nature. "We have used our 'Cludiant,' as you call it, to learn from civilizations across the galaxy. We have even been to your Earth, though not in many millennia." She raised a hand to the wall, where a new image had appeared: a massive marble building with hundreds of steps leading up to an enormous structure with countless columns holding up a massive roof. "At one time on your Earth, we started to build—"

"That's the Library of Alexandria," von Schoor said. She was quickly out of her seat, soon followed by Rhys, standing just short of the image. Both Rhys and von Schoor pulled off their glasses as they tried to study it. "But how?" von Schoor asked. "How do you have a picture of something that was destroyed thousands of years ago?" She reached for the image, though she couldn't touch it. "It's almost like a photograph, not a painting or artistic rendering."

Esfani nodded as more people got up from the table and began to study the image. "It's not so much a photograph. It's a memory of the actual library when it was at its busiest." She smiled, as if that was explanation enough. But Burnaby, von Schoor, and Rhys looked at each other as if they were parched and she was the only source of water for miles.

"Can you explain to us how you know this?" Rhys asked. "How you can have an image of exactly what it looked like before it was destroyed? Not even our extensive knowledge on Earth has information like this about the library."

There was suddenly discussion in the theater above, though Esfani silenced it with a look. She gestured for the scientists to sit, which Rhys reluctantly did. "That it was destroyed is a shame. Knowledge should be shared, and never lost." She got up and moved her chair closer to Rhys and Jason. When she sat, she leaned forward in her seat as she reached out for their hands. "It would be easier to show you than explain it. Would that be okay?" Before either could answer, she turned to Jason. "You truly are of a free spirit," she said to him, which Jason smiled at. However, Rhys was a bit creeped out by it, because that meant she'd taken particular knowledge from Jason's mind while they were all incapacitated. "Would it be okay to share one of your memories with everyone?"

Jason didn't bat an eyelash. "As long as I'm not naked and whatever memory you grab isn't porn related, sure." He winked at Rhys.

Clearly, Jason was much braver than Rhys.

"Very well." Esfani closed her eyes and dipped her head, and the image of the Library of Alexandria disappeared from the wall. In its place was what looked like a video, except it was choppy to the point of nearly making Rhys nauseous. The images painted on the wall looked familiar, and after a few seconds, Rhys realized it was downtown Portland. The sun was shining, though everyone who came into view was wearing sweaters, so that—along with the fallen brown and red leaves piled up along the side of the road—meant it must have been autumn. The image went to a cellphone, where a text message read, *Come to dinner at my place tonight.* The name at the top of the screen was "Paul."

Rhys watched as two thumbs typed out, *Sure. What time?* in response. He sat up a little straighter when the thumbs typed out a kiss. Who the hell was Jason texting a kiss to? Jason had never mentioned a Paul to him.

The image changed slightly when two bells rang through the air, and he watched as

Jason looked up and watched the Portland streetcar come to a stop in front of him. That was followed by a dizzying bundle of movements as Jason bounded up onto the streetcar steps—and promptly fell right at the feet of a familiar pair of shoes.

Rhys knew those shoes. Those were his. The memory Esfani was displaying was the day that Rhys and Jason met. It all felt like such an invasion of privacy that Rhys wanted to tell her to stop. But Jason just smiled as he watched the memory play for everyone to watch, and winked at Rhys when he caught his eye.

For the next few minutes, he watched as the image of memory-Rhys picked up Jason from where he fell up the streetcar steps. Jason looked and saw a few open seats at the front of the streetcar, but purposefully chose to sit next to Rhys. And he continued to watch as Jason made small talk to a bashful looking memory-Rhys.

It was odd to look at himself through Jason's eyes. Though the moment on the screen was almost a decade old, which made Rhys that much younger, he still thought he looked awkward and gangly. Especially as he watched the awkward image of himself making small talk back to Jason, though it warmed his heart when he realized something he'd not known all those years ago. Rhys had made a nerdy, science-based joke, but didn't realize because of the noise at the time that Jason had actually smiled. "Hold on a sec," memory-Jason said, then pulled out his phone. He texted Paul again. *Sorry, but I forgot I already had plans. Mom's in town. Maybe next weekend?* Except this time, there was no kiss emoji. And that somehow made Rhys smile.

Rhys watched as memory-Rhys suddenly blushed, then stood up. "This is me," he said, then went to the door. Once they opened, Rhys stepped out. Jason watched him as he walked away, but stopped and turned just as the doors started to close. Memory-Rhys's voice was low, but he smiled just the same when he remembered what came next. "Oh thank god," memory-Rhys said as Jason parted the doors, pushing his way out of the streetcar and onto the pavement.

"Hey," memory-Jason called as he approached his Rhys. "I don't really do this, but... Would you like to go to dinner some time?" After the briefest of pauses, Jason added, "I mean, you don't have to..."

"I'd love to," memory-Rhys replied, his face split into a wide smile.

As soon as the words were out of Rhys's mouth, the image faded, leaving them again with a blank wall.

Esfani sat back up, released Rhys and Jason's hands, and gave them a perfunctory nod. "There you have it. We have the ability to harness the brain and its memories. But not just a single person's memories."

The room was silent for several seconds until one of the airmen finally spoke up. "Well I don't know about y'all," Darnell Thomas said as he looked around the room, but settled his gaze on Rhys and Jason, "but that just seemed like a gross invasion of privacy." He turned to Esfani. "How can your people use such a tool when it doesn't protect the private thoughts of the people you're pulling them from?" He turned to Rhys and Jason. "Rhys, Jason, pardon me for being so blunt, but right then it looked like Jason was already dating someone when he met Rhys. Jason, I mean no disrespect. But Rhys? Did you know that Jason was making plans with someone else when he met you?"

Rhys was glad he didn't have to bring up the thought, but felt uncomfortable now that it was hanging in the room around them. There were a few more seconds of silence until Jason spoke up. "I never told him," he said to the airman. He turned his gaze to Rhys. "But to be honest, Rhys is different from any person I've ever met. I know a lot of people bandy about the phrase 'love at first sight' like it's nothing. But for me"—he reached out and took Rhys's hand—"it was completely real."

Rhys knew he'd felt the same way from the moment that Jason had sat down next to him on the streetcar. Still, that didn't change the fact that he was embarrassed both because of the privacy of their moment, as well as the jealousy he knew he had no reason to harbor. He tried to let it go, but it felt stuck to his soul like a bad seed.

"So tell me," Rhys finally said as he tried to move on from what had just happened. "Showing a memory from Jason is one thing. But the Library of Alexandria has been gone for thousands of years. How is it you can pull up images of something long gone?"

Esfani just smiled. She got up from where she sat and crossed back to the head of the table. As she put her chin in her hands, she asked, "Do you want to know everything?"

And Rhys did. He did want to know everything. The problem was, a big part of his brain wondered if he was ready for it.

Chapter Nine

"So how does this work?" Rhys asked. He was ready to fully embrace the mantra of 'learn now, deal with the consequences later,' no matter how it went, almost as if the invasion of Jason's privacy hadn't happened. He wanted to learn all he could from Esfani and her people before they left the planet.

But fate stepped in the way. Esfani turned slightly to the side, looked up toward the gallery above, and nodded her head. "I'm sorry," Esfani said as she stood up, "but we'll have to continue this discussion later. I've just been told that your colleague Valentina Palomo has woken up." She turned to Franks. "Captain, would you like me to take you to her?"

Franks looked over at Rhys and Jason, then turned to her two airmen. "Luu, Thomas? Nobody leaves this room. And if someone needs to for any reason, you go as a group.

Understood?"

"Yes, ma'am," the two airmen replied in unison.

Tambra Franks looked around, nodded, and rapped her knuckles on the metallic surface of the table. "See you guys in a bit," she said, then walked out with Esfani.

The room sat in silence for all of ten seconds before it was broken. "Okay," Jason said, just loud enough for the people around him to hear, "I know there's a lot of opportunity to learn here, but seriously." He dropped his voice even lower. "This place is creepy as fuck." A few in the group nodded, while others looked at each other as if trying to explain what had happened. "And don't call me crazy, but I kinda want a tin foil hat to wear around these people." He leaned back in his seat with a smile, but there was still a seriousness to his tone.

"Jase, I'm sorry about..." Rhys didn't finish. Instead, he bobbed his head toward the wall where they had watched the memory of Jason and Rhys meeting for the first time play out.

"No secrets," Jason said to him. He reached out and took Rhys's hand into his own. "Besides, you're way hotter than Paul. And he lied to me about all sorts of stuff—something you'd never do." Jason winked, which caught Rhys off guard because of the secret of the fake charm that he didn't even want to tell Jason about. Hell, he didn't even want to think about it too much, lest the peanut gallery above them have some psychic snoopers in their midst. Maybe Jason's joke about a tin foil hat wasn't too far off.

"I know it's a little creepy and all," von Schoor said, "but honestly, these people can teach us so much about all that they've learned. I mean, they've been documenting everything they've learned for thousands of years, as well as passed it on for future generations. It's a model that I like, even if it means giving up some privacy."

"Do you really mean that?" Jason's bluntness caught Rhys a bit blindsided. "We've seen what giving up privacy means, and how it's negatively affected different aspects of our lives. I don't mean things like agreeing to have the contents of your email read so advertisers can better target you with ads. I mean things like that." He pointed to the wall. "I mean private stuff like that." He shook his head. "Ingrid"—he leaned forward and reached across the table to take the scientist's hands into his own—"what would happen if you wanted to keep your thing with John secret, only to have it splayed out on a giant screen for everyone to watch? I mean, what if it could be used against you? Against him? Not that anyone here would, but there are people out there that live for that kind of crap. They could use it to blackmail you. They could use it to blackmail John, get him kicked out of the Air Force. Get him to kill the project. Hell, the possibilities are endless."

The room sat silent for a moment. "But we should always look to learn and grow as a people," Rhys said. "Shouldn't we?" He hated how his voice squeaked at the end. For the first time in a while, Rhys was unsure of himself. Things had dramatically changed since they'd first entered this room, and now it was far from a sure thing.

He was about to continue the debate when the door opened and Esfani returned. She turned and gestured for Franks, who was followed in by a healthy-looking Airman Palomo. And while Palomo looked vibrant and young as ever, there was a hint of shock hiding in her expression. Most would miss it, but Rhys and Jason knew Palomo better than most. She'd taken them aside early on after her team had migrated to Terra and said that she thought what they were doing was brave. She was more for being in the background, not used to the limelight at all. Though she immediately made them feel old when she said they reminded her of her uncle and his partner, who had been together for going on 30 years.

And then the memories flooded back. The last time Rhys had seen her, she had been laying in a pool of blood, her leg detached.

"How are you feeling?" he asked Airman Palomo as he stood up and pulled her into a hug. "Are you okay?"

Palomo looked around the room as she bit her lip. She looked uncomfortable with all eyes on her, but she stood up a little straighter and nodded. "I'm fine, honestly," she said. "The doctors here... Well, they're amazing." She let go of Rhys and sat down next to Franks. "I don't really remember much of what happened." She closed her eyes as if focusing on a thought, and finally opened them when she began to speak. "I remember seeing her"—she pointed to Esfani— "except she was dressed in pastel-colored robes." She looked at Esfani for a moment, like it was the first time she'd been given a chance to study her. "May I ask, why are you wearing an Air Force uniform with my name stitched across your chest?"

Franks put a protective hand on Palomo's arm. "It's a long story."

Palomo nodded. "Well, I remember you, Captain, telling me to remove all my weapons, and I did. And then as we were walking in, I heard a click, and suddenly remembered the grenade belt on my back. But before I could stop and remove it…" She sank into herself, becoming timid, something Rhys wasn't used to seeing from someone who, while short in stature, could tower over others with her presence when the situation called for it. "And then all I remember was pain—until I woke up in their infirmary."

"Yeah, tell me about that." Franks turned her attention to Esfani. "I mean, it sounded like Valentina here was—if it were any other situation—mortally wounded. But you were able to not only save her life, but reattach her leg." She looked down at Palomo's leg, got the 'okay' to touch it with a questioning look, and gingerly did so. "I mean, it is her own leg, correct?" She asked Palomo to stand up, they moved themselves out of sight for the most part—though Rhys still had a direct view—and Franks requested for Palomo to pull the uniform aside just enough to see the skin at her hips. "I mean, there's barely any way you could tell that her leg was detached." She looked at Esfani. "Your surgeons are that advanced?"

"We have perfected a great number of things." Esfani sat up a little straighter, looking regal. "Remember, we have been doing nothing but learning and research for thousands of years."

Rhys was interested in the research, but more on the receiving end of it and not teetering along the edge, as they had been for the last while. "So how does it work?" he asked, mimicking his question from before. He knew the question was vague, so he tried to clarify as he gestured to Palomo. "I mean, the surgery. Replicating human blood. Reattaching limbs, including all the arteries and nerves. And doing it all in such a way that she was able to walk out of the procedure on her own, just hours later."

"Her kidney, colon, bladder, and lower intestine, and a few other organs as well," Esfani said. "They were damaged in the incident and had to be repaired."

Rhys was in awe of these people's capabilities. He leaned forward, his hands resting on the table in supplication. "Can you teach us?"

"Wait, wait, wait," Burnaby said. "Before we get into"—she shook her hands around, gesturing at both Palomo and Rhys—"all that, let's go back to the beginning. You said your people were on our planet at one time?"

"Indeed." Esfani turned in her chair to the scientist. "Many thousands of years ago."

Rhys, Burnaby, and von Schoor all shared a look.

"How about you start there, then?" Burnaby sat back in her seat, arms crossed. She turned to Rhys. "If that's okay." To which Rhys nodded.

Esfani looked around the room with a smile. "It would be easier to show you, if that would be okay." She pointedly looked at Jason and Rhys, then around the entire room. "By way of explanation, I must begin by asking you a question." She again focused on Burnaby.

"Doctor Sheila Burnaby," she said, then smiled. "That's a family name, isn't it? Sheila?"

"It is," Burnaby replied. "It was my grandmother's name. On my father's side."

"And it was your great-grandmother's name on your mother's side. And again, three generations back from that. And two generations back again on your father's side."

There was a quick murmur around the room. "How would you know that?" Burnaby asked. "Even I don't know that. And they're my family."

"These"—Esfani pulled the charm from around her neck—"are more than just a key to get you from planet to planet. And the Cludiant, as you call it, is so much more than just a means of transport. When you first came to this planet, we were able to tell what planet you came from, your genomic makeup, your medical issues, blood type, and all manner of other information. That is why we had Valentina Palomo's blood and duplicates of her vital organs available. Because of our automatic defensive weapons, we have made it a standard practice to manufacture backup items in case of need."

"But isn't that a waste?" Rhys asked.

"It is better to be prepared. But yes, most often things have gone to waste. However, we have an abundance of supplies for making these things, so why not have them just in case?"

While the room was silent, Rhys caught Palomo flinch out of the corner of his eye.

"Tell me, Doctor Sheila Burnaby," Esfani said as she gathered everyone's attention again. "You have the memory of your parents, correct?"

"Yes," Burnaby replied. "Although my father died when I was in high school."

Esfani nodded. "And your parents. They had their own memories, as well as the memories of their parents, right? And continuing back generation after generation?"

Several people around the table shared confused looks.

"Yes, in theory," Burnaby replied. "But my mother died a couple years ago, so I don't have access to her to ask her things anymore."

"Oh, but you do."

A murmur bounced around the room, and it again went utterly silent.

"You mean like a séance?" Jason asked.

With a sickly-sweet smile, Esfani put her hand on Jason's arm. "No, little one."

Jason sat up with a start and instantly pulled his hand away. He looked as if he wanted to get as far from the table as possible.

"Did I do something wrong?" Esfani asked. "That is what your grandparents called you, isn't it?"

Jason got up and paced around the back of the room.

"Jase?" Rhys got up and went to Jason's side. He slipped an arm around Jason's waist and tucked him close. "Are you okay?"

It took Jason a second to come back to himself. He finally nodded, then wiped a stray tear from his face and kissed Rhys gently on the cheek. "Yeah," he said as Rhys led him back to the chair to sit back down. "It's just... Nobody's

ever called me that. Not since Grandpa died."
He reached over and squeezed Rhys's hand. He
took a deep breath and gave Rhys a weak smile
as he wiped away another stray tear. "So these,"
he said as he pulled the charm from around his
neck with his free hand and showed it to Esfani.
"These somehow let you access your parents'
memories, and their parents'? All the way back
to…"

Esfani nodded. She turned to the blank
wall, where the stark white was quickly replaced
with a fuzzy image that took a few seconds to
come into focus. "These images are coming
from the memories of my family, who was there
when the Library of Alexandria, as you called it,
was flourishing. But the memories should not
come just from me," she said as more and more
detail painted itself in the image. She looked
around the room and pointed. "They're also
coming from your ancestors, Miss Palomo. Your
ancestors, Mister Thomas. And your ancestors."
She looked at Rhys and Jason, and was taken
aback. "It's actually the same ancestor."

Rhys's mind went back to the hot summer day in the lab outside of Sacramento when he found out that his nineteenth great grandmother was also Jason's twentieth great grandmother. "Yeah, we found out about that last year," Rhys said. "But that was twenty generations ago."

"Ahh." Esfani nodded back and forth.

They turned their attention back to the image painted against the wall as it came alive, bustling with people and animals. Then, slowly, the image separated into two distinct images, then three, and then four. The library itself was the commonality at the beginning. But that image faded as individual memories started to paint themselves across the blank canvas, showing the different aspects of life in ancient Alexandria. Esfani's memories, no doubt, were the ones depicted on the screen showing the inside of the library with scrolls and tablets. There were odd-looking machines, hieroglyphics, and people buzzing around, keeping busy. Another section stayed mostly outside the library, showing wares for sale. The last two looked to be the lives of slaves, based on the dusty, dirty work being shown.

"What was his name?" Airman Thomas asked.

"Darcaue," Esfani replied. "He was a proud man who eventually led a slave rebellion against his captors. He was beheaded as punishment." She said the last part quite matter-of-factly, which caused several of the group to start.

They watched the images play out for a few more seconds until they softened, finally replaced by the solid white wall. Rhys had been fascinated. Not just by the images of an important part of Earth's history, but also by the fact that they had the technology to harness immense energy. This could revolutionize almost every single aspect of life on Earth, not to mention everything that they could learn about scientific and surgical techniques that could end disease and solve countless problems that the Earth was facing. And maybe even make their migration to Terra that much easier.

"So these shared memories—do you use this primarily for learning? For education?" Rhys wanted to know everything.

"Not just learning, no," Esfani replied. "We use it for so much more, like the planetwide dissemination of important information. We use it to share events that others have missed, from someone's birthday to a loved one's life celebration." She clasped her hands together and smiled. "But we also use it for entertainment."

"What, like showing someone's private memories for the amusement of others?" There was a little heat hidden in Airman Thomas's words; he was clearly not over what had happened earlier.

"Nothing like that, my dear." Esfani leaned toward Palomo, who instinctively leaned away from her. "I'm going to pick on you a little," she said, "since your captain so graciously shared a secret with us." She gave an innocent smile, then reached out and took

Franks's hand on one side and Jason's on the other. "Though this works better if we all join hands, instead of displaying it."

Franks turned to Thomas and Luu and shook her head. "You two sit this one out," she said, her voice innocuous. But Rhys knew the captain well enough to understand she didn't wholly trust Esfani.

"Close your eyes," Esfani said, and Rhys did as she requested. As he did, a flash appeared behind his eyelids, and suddenly an entire movie seemed to play out in the span of a second. It started with a young girl, who couldn't have been more than six or seven, putting on a pair of ballerina shoes for the first time. It showed her practicing, getting better as she aged, and finished with her dancing on a stage with bravos called loudly from the audience and flowers thrown at her feet.

As quickly as the image appeared, it stopped, and Rhys opened his eyes.

"That," Jason said, then sputtered. "That was amazing." As they all released hands, he turned to Esfani. "This is what your planet does for entertainment?"

"Among other things," she said. "Quite often, our poets and our writers say that language is not always able to properly convey the emotion that sometimes hides behind their words. So instead of working the traditional way, they will share their visions with the audience like this. It still allows for an emotional connection and conveys what they are trying to say. Just without words."

Rhys sat in wonder. "Is there anything you Comperians can't do?"

"Comperian?" Palomo asked. "Oh," she said as she gently shook her head, as if she had finally solved an ancient riddle. "Is that derived from the Latin 'comperior?'" Then she turned to Franks, then Rhys. "It means 'to discover.'"

A small smile again appeared on Esfani's face. She looked up at the gallery above, then gave a barely discernable nod. "Actually," she said, "you're very close to the truth. Only that it doesn't come from Latin. You can say that Latin comes from us." She looked at Rhys and nodded. "We brought it to your planet."

All three scientists immediately started throwing questions at Esfani, and she threw up her hands as if to quiet the group. "I can explain," she said as the voices died down. When it was finally quiet again, she said, "And I will explain it all. But now that you are all here"—she gestured to Palomo—"I again have to ask you, do you want to know everything?"

Rhys smiled. But before he could respond, Captain Franks dropped a heavy hand onto the table. "Absolutely not!"

Chapter Ten

Chaske Oglala had been on just about every single news, opinion, and talk show in the last two months, usually with the like-minded Emily Bradley. He considered himself a man of action, not of talking points and studio lights, and felt like he got more done behind the scenes than in front of the camera. But he wanted to get his message out, and if that meant having to do news programs, then so be it. He was willing to spend time in the artificial reality of a television studio to sacrifice for the planet he loved.

After his last appearance, he made his way back home. It was no surprise that when the cameras were off he sought downtime with his roots. Gone too long, he started to crave the connection to his people, his community, the Earth. That was what really mattered to him. So after a week full of contentious appearances, Chaske decided to go back to his home in

Oklahoma and spend some time where he thought he could do more good than he had been.

"Rack 'em up," he said as he walked into the saloon, a big smile on his face. All of his buddies were there, and he instantly felt himself begin to recharge amongst the dimly lit and smoke-filled interior. After saying his hellos, he offered to buy a round of drinks for his friends. But as he approached the bar, the bartender pointed his thumb over his shoulder, so Chaske looked at the other side of the bar.

"Chaske," the bartender said, then bobbed his head again. "Somebody here to see you." He finished wiping the pint glass, then put it in the cooler, ready for use.

"Round for my boys." Chaske rapped twice on the counter.

When the bartender acknowledged him, Chaske nodded and walked to the other side of the bar. He found a couple people seated together, carrying on in a low conversation which was mostly drowned out by the tinny, twangy country music coming from the saloon's ancient jukebox. They were dressed like they were from the government, most likely, at least based on the woman who sat in the booth. She looked professional yet cold, with her hair pulled back in a severe bun. The two men with her seemed inconsequential—more like bodyguards than anything else. Chaske wondered if they were military.

"Mister Oglala," the woman said as she dismissed her companions. The two men got up and walked away, giving them some privacy. She gestured for the open bench. "Please, sit."

Chaske stood there, his arms crossed over his massive chest as he sized her up. "What do you want?" he asked, intent on not moving from where he stood.

"I've seen several of your television interviews." She coolly took a sip of her drink. "You've made some very persuasive arguments on shutting down the Migration project."

At least someone had been watching. "What about it?"

The woman stared at him for a moment before removing a folder from her briefcase and putting it on the table, tapping it with a well-manicured nail. The brown folder was thick with loose papers and newspaper clippings. She pulled out a few of the clippings, with multiple pictures of a younger Chaske under sensationalized headlines splayed out across the pages. "You are a man of action." It was almost enough to bring a smile to Chaske's face. Still, he figured the woman was probably just feeding his ego, so he remained cautious. "Why waste your time with words in front of a camera when you have taken action and gotten so much more accomplished?"

Chaske knew the clippings and reports very well—they were a portrait of his youth. Though he had been just sixteen at the time, Chaske had successfully run a program of sabotage and subterfuge when it was announced an oil pipeline was to be built on Native lands. The program had been rushed through government channels, bypassing safety and concerns by those whose land it was to be built on—land that was sacred to Chaske and his people. But a project of its size was no match for Chaske and his rowdy bunch of friends. For every day of progress the oil company made, Chaske and his group put them further and further behind in schedule. And for every milestone the oil company met, Chaske and his team destroyed as much of the company's property as possible, making them restart over and over again.

"What is that old saying? The squeaky wheel gets the grease." Chaske studied the woman as he tried to figure out what she wanted from him.

"Indeed," the woman replied. "My family has a vested interest in stopping the Cludiant project, no matter the cost." She ran her fingers over the documentation, her fingernail tapping against the word *TEEN* printed in a tall, thin font. "If you can get this much done at just sixteen with limited resources, well"—she sat back in the booth with a smile on her face. It was an almost unnerving smile, with coldness and a hint of danger behind it—"what might you be able to do today, now that you've grown older and wiser? And with my family's considerable wealth behind you."

Chaske looked over the table and pulled out one of the pictures he'd been most proud of. It was him, face bloodied by a hired goon's fist, being led away in handcuffs. It was the day that the project had finally been scuttled. After all, it wasn't good PR for the oil company after armed guards battled with teenagers, leaving many battered and bruised. The negative media attention had finally brought about the end of the project and secured a huge win for Chaske and his people.

After a moment, Chaske dropped the photograph on the table and pulled at the waist of his pants as he sat down. "And what family is that, Miss…"

"Bartlett." The woman held out her hand. "Delia Bartlett." They sat in silence for a few moments too long. "As for the family," she said, shaking her head gently, "that's none of your concern. Instead, let's focus on what you would like to do with this Migration project, and how best to shut it down."

As Chaske considered her request, he scratched at the whiskers on his chin. "Might need to round up a small army," he said. "We'll need supplies. Plans. Time to figure out how the project is working now so we can understand their weaknesses." The bartender came over and dropped off his beer, which he took, raised in cheer, then took a sip. As he put the frosted glass on the table, he added, "That's going to take some major funds."

"That won't be a problem," Bartlett replied. "We'll cover it."

"Good." Chaske took another sip. "When would you like to start?"

Bartlett leaned close and gave him another creepy smile. "When can you be available for us to fly you to Sacramento?"

Chapter Eleven

The room had gone still for several seconds as all eyes landed on Captain Franks. No one moved for what felt like the longest time until Rhys turned to Franks. "What do you mean, 'absolutely not?'" He knew his voice sounded defensive, but so be it. Who was Franks to scuttle their chance at learning? Esfani and her people held the secrets to the universe—knowledge that would help them end pain and hunger on Earth. Knowledge that would help them migrate to Terra more efficiently. Knowledge of peace and of thousands of other civilizations that they had interacted with for thousands of years. He wondered how it was even a question worth asking.

Instead of answering him, Captain Franks turned to Esfani. "I'm sorry. And not to be an ungrateful guest," she said, "but would it be possible for me to speak to my team? In private?"

Esfani looked at Franks, then Rhys, and finally stood. "As you wish." She looked up toward the gallery above, and Rhys watched as the glass turned translucent. Then with a nod, she was quickly out the door. It was still odd to see her in the Air Force uniform. But a part of Rhys's brain knew that it would be harder telling her no, because the outfit just made it feel like they were separating a member from the team. Rhys shook his head to get his thinking straight again.

It wasn't until several seconds later, after the noises in the nearby hallway died down, that Franks turned to Rhys. "Doctor Tambor," she began. But that was as far as she got before Rhys started in.

"What's going on, Captain?" He knew it was petty to use his friend's rank, but it was to counter her formal use of his name. Franks rarely called him 'Doctor Tambor'—usually only when she wanted to grab his attention during a rant, or when he was so engaged with other scientists that he didn't realize whatever situation they were in had boiled up into something bigger than he'd expected. "I mean, come on! There is so much we can learn from these people. Just..." He was at a complete loss for words, because she'd been there for everything. He sputtered for a second, grounded when Jason stood up and put a finger through his belt loop. "I mean, look at Valentina," he continued. "These people saved her life. Shouldn't we at least listen to them to see how they did it?"

"Rhys." Palomo's voice was barely louder than a whisper. "There's things..." she said, then shook her head. "When I was in their infirmary, there were things going on. Things with those little round creatures." She closed her eyes and shook her head. "We need to talk about it, but not here."

"What happened?" Rhys said, just as Franks asked, "What's going on, Palomo?"

But before the airman could respond, Esfani slipped back into the room, once again wearing the pastel-colored robes that she'd been dressed in, her long, black hair once again flowing past her shoulders. She looked around the room, then turned her focus on Franks. "I take it you do not have an agreement between your team members?"

Franks's brow bunched up as she considered Esfani for a moment. "Are you reading out thoughts? Or…"

Esfani's expression lightened as she took her seat. "No, no," she said. "Not without permission, I wouldn't. What I mean is, even just walking into the room, I can feel what you might call an 'aura' of uncertainty and unease coming off several of you, while only a couple of you seem to be okay with moving ahead."

Captain Franks nodded. She looked around, and Rhys could feel Jason pulling on his belt loop once again until he leaned back in his seat and relaxed a bit. It was just a small gesture, but again, Jason knew how to walk Rhys back from the precipice like no other person. Rhys allowed himself to take a deep breath and shake off some of the nervous energy that had taken hold.

It was then that Franks looked at Rhys, concern in her eyes. But Rhys understood where she was coming from. Even if he didn't like it. As he let go of a deep breath, he nodded slightly to Franks, who nodded back with the barest hint of a smile on her face. After a slow blink, they turned back to their host.

"Esfani," she said, smiling at the woman, "it is no secret that we are deeply in debt to you and your people for saving our colleague. And we very much would like to learn everything that you've shown us today. But"—she shook her head—"today is just not that day." She stood up a little straighter. "After all, today was just supposed to be a meet-and-greet. That's all. We honestly were not prepared for such an event. What I would like to do is go back to our planet to make a plan with our project leadership. And then, when the time is appropriate, we would like to come back and visit you, but with many more scientists than just the few we have today. Specialists in surgery and medicine and physics, and whatever else you can teach us. This is truly an honor, but we aren't ready yet."

Rhys understood why Franks was telling Esfani this. He didn't have to like it, though, because he genuinely wanted to learn. But no doubt when they came back, he would be the first one through the Cludiant to greet Esfani and her people.

"Very well." Esfani stood up from the table, her expression curious. "I'm sorry to hear that you are not ready. We will allow you to travel back to your planet, but not all of you."

There was suddenly a cacophony of voices, topped only when Franks yelled, "Quiet!" and stepped close to Esfani. "What do you mean, not all of us?"

"Doctor Tambor and his husband. Valentina Palomo. Darnell Thomas." Each name was said matter-of-factly, without any malice, even if the plans hidden by her words were filled with nothing but. "The rest of you are dismissed.

These four will stay with us."

"Why?" Rhys asked as Franks said, "Why do you want to hold my team?"

"Because we are not finished with them," Esfani replied. "You saw." She pointed to the wall, where the images of each of their parents painted themselves for all to see. "We have determined that there is information within them that we need. They will stay with us until we are done, at which time they will rejoin you on your planet."

"Now just a second." Franks was out of her seat and right into Esfani's face, who seemed, for the most part, completely unfazed. "We are a team. We come in as a group and we leave as a group. When we leave, they will come with us."

Rhys's face flushed as a cold feeling settled into the pit of his stomach.

Esfani's cold eyes showed no emotion. "This is not negotiable," she said, her voice clinical.

"You're right. It's not," Franks said.

"Thomas? Luu? Get the civilians out of here. Palomo? You're with me."

Luu grabbed Rhys and Jason by their shirts and pulled them toward the door, as Thomas did the same to von Schoor and Burnaby. Just as they reached the door, Esfani shook her head. "I'm truly sorry," she said, "but you leave me no choice."

Esfani raised her hands and opened her mouth. Suddenly there was blackness at the side of his vision, and he watched as each member of his team fell to the ground. She calmly said in Rhys's mind, "You'll understand," as she focused on his eyes. The look of a madman gazed back at him, though he felt helpless to do anything about it. As the darkness closed around him, he closed his eyes and silently slipped into unconsciousness.

Chapter Twelve

Rhys slowly began to come to, but the more he opened his eyes, the more his head hurt. There was something off about where he was, though his head hurt too much to consider what might be causing it. He could barely open his eyes, and it took entirely too much effort to raise his hand to shield his face. Memories of Esfani and their adventure to Comperian flooded his mind, and from what he could tell, he was still on the planet, but now in a stark-white, blazingly bright room. Even what little light that bled through his eyelids was too much. Beyond that, it even hurt to breathe, though that was nothing compared to the pain he felt in his temple. Whatever hangover headache this was, it was nothing like any pain he had experienced before. He rubbed a finger up and down between his eyes, but his brain continued to throb.

When he was finally able to concentrate

on his breathing, Rhys managed to open his eyes the tiniest amount. There was a figure in the corner, though it hurt him too much whenever he tried to focus. But it didn't take too much to figure out who it was. The figure had a bird's nest of dirty-blond hair—a mess of hair that he would recognize anywhere. "Jase?"

The room was silent for a beat, and it stretched when Jason didn't respond. Rhys opened his eyes a little more.

"Rhys?" Jason finally replied.

He didn't know what Esfani or the Comperian people had done to them, but they had been knocked unconscious once again. They had to find a way to avoid that if they were ever going to get off the planet. "Are you okay?" Rhys asked.

"I'm fine," Jason replied, his voice flat.

"Don't you feel... I dunno, wasted? Or like you've been run over?" Rhys managed to crawl closer to where Jason sat against a bright white wall. And while it was still entirely too bright, the coolness of the wall was a comfort against Rhys's back. He turned to Jason, but it still hurt too much to focus on him.

It looked like Jason might have shrugged, based on what little Rhys could make out. "Whatever that was must have hit you harder than me," was all Jason said.

Rhys didn't know how that was even possible. Every joint in his body ached, and his head felt like it'd been severed and reattached. Several times. He tried to focus, but every time he did, shooting pains began at his temple, and a warm, burning sensation hit him behind his eyes.

After a strange silence stretched between them, Rhys finally said, "When I'm feeling up to it, we need to figure out where we are and how we can get out of here." He tried to focus his thoughts, then reached out and touched Jason on the arm. But what he found was cold. "Jason? Are you okay?" He gripped tighter, though Jason didn't move.

"What did you mean back there?" Jason asked, ignoring Rhys's question.

Rhys thought for a moment. "Mean back

where?" He turned to Jason, but was still unable to open his eyes farther without excruciating pain. "What are you talking—"

"Back in the room," Jason replied. "You said some gibberish word. What did it mean?"

Rhys dropped his hand from Jason's side. "Gibberish?"

"You know," Jason continued, "the one Esfani asked you about. You said that it was just something you and I would say to each other, but I can't remember you ever saying anything like that to me."

The pain at Rhys's temple grew and throbbed along with his heartbeat. But even though he was in pain, Jason seemed to be immune. And what was Jason asking, anyway? It was like…

"Jason?" he asked. "Where did we meet?"

He could see well enough to know that Jason had turned to him, dark, soulless eyes staring back at him. "What does it mean?" Jason asked again.

"And I'm asking, where did we meet?" Something was completely off.

"Portland Streetcar. Northwest 13th & Lovejoy. Earth."

It wasn't that Jason's voice was clinical. It was the completely unnecessary addition of their home planet that caught Rhys off guard.

Rhys fought against the pain and opened his eyes. But the more he did, the brighter it became. He continued to fight, even as the light grew more intense. He began to stand, leaning against the wall to brace himself as much to help him stand as well as to stanch the pain that continued to grow inside him.

"This isn't real," he said.

He inched up the wall, bracing his forehead against it.

"This isn't real," he repeated.

It seemed like it took hours, but he finally stood on his own power, though he still needed to lean against the wall for strength. "This isn't real."

A voice came from what sounded like

every direction. Jason's voice. "What does it mean?"

"This isn't real. This isn't real. This isn't—"

Rhys opened his eyes. It hadn't been real. None of it. He began to come to, and as he did, realized there was a bright light and hum coming from just above him. He was on a bed with scratchy blankets under him and had something strapped to his forehead. He raised a hand and brushed it off, letting it clatter to the tiled floor below. The light immediately dimmed, and the thrum of pain quickly dissipated, replaced with the barest hint of a dull ache. As his eyes adjusted, he realized he was in a darkened room, laying on a cot. He lay there quietly as a wave of nausea passed over him, and when he was able, he leaned up on his arms and swung his legs off the bed. He looked around and realized he wasn't alone. Several beds surrounded him, though only three were occupied.

He got up, wobbly as a newborn calf,

and held onto the bedframe until he had his strength back. When his eyes fully adjusted, he looked over the other three occupied beds. Thomas and Palomo were closest to him. And in the next row lay Jason. Each of them had a glowing charm strapped to their foreheads, an expression of pain painted across each face.

Chapter Thirteen

The ride to Sacramento wasn't the first time Chaske had been on an airplane. Wasn't even the first time he'd been on an aircraft that week. It was, however, the first time he'd been on a private jet. He'd spent most of the journey looking out the window, sipping on a single beer, making it last the entire three-hour flight.

As he walked down the air stairs, Chaske was surprised to find Bartlett waiting for him. She gave him a perfunctory smile before gesturing to a helicopter, the rotor blades already slicing through the air. He followed her into the back seat of the aircraft and put on the helmet, which contained earphones and a microphone, before strapping in. "Where's this thing going that that thing can't?" He pointed to the jet.

Bartlett didn't respond at once. She took her time putting on a pair of sunglasses, then keyed the microphone. "We can't fly over the base where they're keeping the Cludiant, so this'll have to do." She made a couple adjustments, then keyed again. "We'll blend in with news crews flying overhead, shooting video of those migrating."

Before Chaske could reply, the helicopter lifted off. It felt like he was leaving his stomach along with the pavement, and it took him a few seconds to gather himself.

"You get used to it," Bartlett said.

Within just a few minutes, the helicopter began to slow and positioned itself on the perimeter of what looked like a row of barracks—dull, brown rows of minimalistic buildings, each one looking exactly like the last.

"See the group of people?" Bartlett leaned forward and pointed out the side of the aircraft. Chaske followed her gaze until he saw what looked like several hundred people, many on foot, but the vast majority on horses, or at least on horse-drawn carriages. It looked like something Chaske had seen when people talked about the Amish. A simple people that lived as close to nature as possible, much like his ancestors had. "Watch them. As they continue to walk, they all seem to go into that building over there." She pointed to another nondescript building maybe a third of a mile from where the line ended. "That's where they're keeping the Cludiant."

A fighter jet buzzed the area, which told Chaske that attack from the air was probably moot. A second jet crossed behind it. Then a third.

He turned his attention back to the ground. "So that's our target."

Bartlett shook her head as she showed him the microphone trigger.

He hit it and repeated himself.

This time, Bartlett nodded. "Now that you know where it is, you need to think about how you want to go about it."

They hovered around the perimeter of the base for a few more minutes until Chaske turned and nodded.

Bartlett signaled to the pilots to head

back to the airport, then sat back in the seat. They made the rest of the trip in silence.

Chaske took his helmet off. "What can you tell me about the Cludiant?" he asked. "How it works. How many personnel you have on the inside. What kind of firepower you can provide." He smiled. "And when do you want it done?"

It was Bartlett's turn to smile as she followed him back onto the pavement. A car drove up, and the driver got out to open the door for them. Bartlett gestured, so Chaske got in first. Once they settled in, the driver got back in and they got underway. "Where're we going?"

"Your apartment." She eased back into the seat. "We'll go over logistics, and then I'll let you come up with your plans. You just need to tell me what or who you need, and give me enough time to get them for you."

Chaske smiled as a plan began to unfold in his brain. This was going to be intriguing.

Chapter Fourteen

It took a second for Rhys to come back to himself. He wasn't sure what was going on with the others, but he was confident that whatever alternate reality they were in, Esfani and her minions were gathering the information she wanted from them. He just hoped that Jason and his friends weren't in the same amount of pain he was.

He walked to Jason's side and found a mix of emotions on his husband's face; the pain and concern continuously plastered across Jason's features made Rhys's stomach turn over. After a second of studying the item on Jason's forehead, he realized that it was just another pendant. Granted, it wasn't any charm that they had seen yet. The more he studied it, the more he realized that it was actually quite plain: triangular, without any holes or description along the front like the one that Jason wore at his neck. Rhys figured that it was probably just the raw material, molded and used by the Comperians for whatever nefarious reason they could think to extract data from their captives.

"Here goes nothing," he muttered, brushing the charm from Jason's forehead. Then he waited.

After what seemed like half a lifetime, Jason bolted up in bed as he gasped for breath.

"Jase? Jase! It's okay. It's all right. It's okay." He sat next to his husband and pulled Jason to him as his breathing slowly steadied. It seemed like forever until Jason shook his head and sighed. When he felt comfortable, Rhys leaned back and looked Jason in the eyes. "Are you okay?"

"Yeah." Jason raised a hand to Rhys's face, which Rhys couldn't help but lean into, enjoying the touch of his husband. "Oh god," he said, then finally relaxed. He kissed Rhys, and they leaned their foreheads together. "God, that was awful."

"Could you tell it was a simulation?"

Rhys asked. "What were they trying to get from you?"

Jason looked into his eyes as a laugh tumbled from his chest. "Oh, no doubt," he said. "I was able to tell almost from the start." He smiled at Jason. "It was you, by the way."

"Me?"

"Yeah," Jason replied. "They used something that looked like you to ask me a bunch of questions. About you. Earth. Terra. My family's history with the Cludiant."

"How did you get out of it?"

The smile on Jason's face grew even more prominent. "Would you believe that the you they constructed in whatever reality that was became even more flustered when I flirted with him?"

That took Rhys aback. "Wait, flirted?"

Jason stood up from the bed, pulling Rhys with him. "Don't worry, baby. I was thinking about you the whole time." He winked.

Rhys laughed. It was truly something that, even during the most stressful times, Jason had a way of making him feel more at ease. It must have been some sort of gift.

"He was more bendy, too," Jason said.

"Bendy?"

Jason winked at him, then gave him another kiss. "I'll tell you about it later." Rhys followed his gaze as Jason looked around, then gestured to their sleeping teammates. "First, let's get these two out from whatever spell these bastards have them under."

*
**

It took a few minutes to get Thomas and Palomo out from under the influence of the charms, as well as bring them up to speed as to what was going on. "What happened to your glasses?" Palomo asked when she was fully back with them.

Rhys took his glasses off and looked at them, but didn't notice anything until Jason pointed to a crack at the top of one of the lenses.

"They're a little busted," he said as Rhys put them back on. "You must have gone down hard."

Thomas was even more out of it than Palomo. And when he was back to his regular self, the muscles at his jawline tensed; Rhys could tell he was furious, so he reached out and put a hand on the airman's shoulder. "Thanks," Thomas said, then gave him a nod. After a deep breath, he asked, "Where are the others?" He looked around, so Rhys explained what was going on. It was then that Rhys saw the shine of something against Thomas's forehead, hidden by the dimmed light of the room. Blood.

He tore a piece of the bedding and dabbed it against Thomas's bleeding forehead, then handed it to the airman. "You okay?" Rhys asked as Thomas held the cloth to his forehead.

"I'm fine," Thomas said through a scowl. "Just pissed off that they gassed us again. Or whatever they did."

"Yeah, what is that, boo?" Jason asked. "Any clue?"

It wasn't too difficult a question, but Rhys still had a problem considering it. "They must be able to... I don't know. Raise our melatonin levels or something?" These people, whom Rhys had deemed brilliant, had a nasty way of getting what they wanted, no matter the cost to others. He looked at Palomo, whose expression was blank.

She sat against the head of the small bed, her legs pulled up and her arms wrapped around her knees. "There's something wrong with those people. And not just because they've almost killed me once, gassed us twice, and now kidnapped and separated us from the rest of the group."

Rhys looked at Jason, who looked as confused as he was.

"What do you mean?" Jason asked.

"Those... Those little round beings we saw when we first got here." She shook her head, crossing her arms over her chest. "Esfani and her people are slaughtering them."

A sudden pit of cold formed in Rhys's

stomach. "What do you mean, slaughtering?"

Palomo shook her head again, a haunting look in her eyes. "When I was in surgery, the surgeons who were operating on me had to wake me up. I was under some sort of nerve block so that I couldn't feel anything. It almost felt like I was floating over myself, looking down and watching the surgery." She shook her head again. "By then, my leg had been reattached, but they were still working on my stomach. I didn't know what they were saying—"

"Wait," Rhys said. "Why couldn't you understand them? The charms act as a universal translator, so you should have been able to understand everything they said."

"You might have, but..." Palomo turned her gloved wrist over. She loosened a strap and opened a small compartment, pulling out the Cludiant charm that was the key between Terra and Comperian. "I don't like wearing the charms around my neck like you guys," she said, "so I keep it in here. As soon as we get to a planet, I unhook the charm after I go through the Cludiant and tuck it in here. That way I always have it nearby, but don't have the skin irritation or pulling sensations you get when you wear it around your neck."

Rhys automatically raised his hand to his neck and tangled his fingers in the chain, then dragged them over the charm. "That makes sense, then," he said. "I mean, that you remember the accident like I do." He looked around, making sure they were alone, but still he lowered his voice. "This is the fake charm that General Landingham made for Jason back when the military had all the pieces of the Cludiant and had just figured out how everything worked. They made this to exactly match the one Jason had so that they could lock the original one up for safety."

"So that's why your little mind wipe didn't work," Jason said. "Jesus, can you imagine what would have happened if we'd had enough of these to go around?" He couldn't help but play with the pendant at his neck until a surprised look overtook his face. "Oh, so that's what you couldn't tell me out there." He grinned at Rhys, then gave him a quick wink. "God, you're smart."

Jason leaned over, bumped Rhys's shoulder, and followed up with a quick kiss on the cheek. As he leaned back, his eyes darted to both Thomas and Palomo. "Sorry, guys." He turned to the airman and gestured for her to continue. "Then what happened?"

"I kind of sat back and watched as they were cleaning up bits and pieces, and then the surgeon barked some sort of order—at least, that's what it sounded like. Then a few seconds later, one of the little translucent guys—"

"Illeuke," Rhys said. "The Comperians called them Illeuke."

"Well, one of the Illeuke rolled itself over and was raised onto a table by an assistant. The surgeon took some sort of tool and cut the Illeuke into two pieces, reached in, and scooped out this…thing. It was either a kidney or my stomach, or something."

"They use them to grow and harvest organs?" Rhys asked.

"Oh my god." Jason reached out and grabbed Rhys's arm. "Remember what Esfani said? They're a part of everyday life. They couldn't do a great many things without the benefit of the Illeuke's existence." Jason shivered, a look of disgust on his face. "Oh god, I feel so dirty." He leaned in close to Rhys. "Boo, these people are kinda horrible."

Jason was right: these people were indeed horrible. "Remember when Esfani said that every time someone comes through the Cludiant, their genetic makeup is examined, and they make 'backup items' and throw out what they don't need?" Rhys shuddered at the thought. "That must mean they use the Illeuke as disposable incubators who get slaughtered when they're needed, and slaughtered when they're of no use to them anymore."

The foursome looked at each other until one of them finally said, "We gotta get outta here."

"Yeah, but how?" Thomas asked. "It doesn't look like there's any door. Just rows and rows of these cots."

Rhys turned to Jason and gave him a curious look.

"What?" Jason asked.

Rhys cocked his head to the side, then looked at Jason. "Wasn't there…" He closed his eyes and concentrated while he tried to pull something from his memory. "In a room with no doors, there's no need for a lock."

"Oh, Grandpa," Jason said, which got confused looks from Thomas and Palomo. "It's something my grandfather used to say all the time. 'In a room absent a door, there's no need for a lock.'" He closed his eyes, then continued. "You've got to sit on the floor the way of the cock. And while you may crow, all you need know is use all your might to push the right block."

They each stood silent for a moment. "So, what? Your grandfather was here?" Thomas asked. "But how is that even possible? I

179

mean, you didn't even find the Cludiant until a few months ago."

"Grandpa had a ton of stories that he passed down to me," Jason said. "I have no idea if this one applies to this planet. It's just something that he used to say as part of the stories." He looked around, putting his hands on his hips. "And I mean, we are in a room without a door. And if you don't have a door, there's no need for a lock."

"Yeah, well I'll leave the cock part to you boys." Palomo gave an impish wink as she crossed her arms again. It was enough to ease the tension just a touch.

"Not that kind of cock," Rhys said. "Or at least, I don't think so. I mean, I think what it means is something about the east side of the room." When everyone gave him an incredulous look, he added, "You know, roosters? Crowing at the rising sun?"

"Dear?" Jason asked, voice full of sarcasm as he shook his head. "I don't know if you've noticed or not, but we currently don't know which way is east on this planet."

Rhys stood there, speechless for a moment. "Oh," he finally said, then rubbed his face in his hands. "Well, that's not helpful."

"Okay, so everybody spread out and see what we can find," Palomo said.

But before they could separate, a mechanical sound came from one side of the room as the walls on the far end somehow began expanding. Thomas and Palomo pushed Rhys and Jason behind them, a gesture Rhys was growing more used to the more time he spent with their military teammates. But what was new was Palomo pulling what looked like a scalpel from her boot. "What is that?" he asked the diminutive airman.

Palomo tilted the blade so it caught the light. "Stole it from the infirmary," she replied, not looking back at Rhys. Instead, her eyes focused on whatever might be coming toward them from the hallway.

A section of the far wall finished rising into the ceiling, and two figures stepped into the entryway. But instead of coming into the room, they stopped short of coming close enough to reveal themselves.

"Stay behind us," Palomo warned.

There was no movement or sound for the longest time. But after a few seconds, the two shapes near the opening became clearer. It didn't take long for them to come closer, and for Rhys to figure out that it was two female Comperians, dressed in flowing robes like Esfani had been when the team had first spotted her. They looked identical, and even stepped in synchrony. The two stopped at the end of the hallway and studied the group, curious expressions on their faces.

"What do you want from us?" Rhys yelled.

Thomas and Palomo automatically pushed him and Jason back.

One of the beings began to raise her arms, much like Esfani had twice before, when she'd twice forced the entire team into unconsciousness.

Palomo darted her gaze to Thomas for a split second, whispering, "Protect them." She flipped the stolen blade in her hand to a defensive grip. After a beat, she breathed out a heavy sigh. Finally, she raised the scalpel, lowered her head, and began to lunge as Thomas stutter-stepped next to her.

Palomo made it a few steps down the hallway at breakneck speed, determined to protect them from the Comperians. But it was Jason's voice which stopped her mid-stride when he screamed, "PALOMO, WAIT!"

Chapter Fifteen

The look on the librarians' eyes went from curious to horrified as Palomo charged at them, the sharpened blade held steady above her head, ready to strike. But Jason caught everyone off guard when he yelled for Palomo to stop, and she nearly tripped as she came to a halt. Before her, the two librarians reached for one another, each one pushing the other behind for protection.

The hallway stood stock still. The only sound that Rhys could hear was the thunderous beat of his heart in his chest. It beat so loud, so strong, he knew the others must be able to hear it.

Seconds later, it was the thumping of Palomo's boots against the floor that finally broke the silence. As she lowered the scalpel to her side, she asked, "What?" She glanced back at the two librarians and took a step back. Not that either of them looked brave enough to take on an Air Force airman.

"Didn't you hear them?" Jason asked. But as soon as the words came out of his mouth, he slapped his forehead. "Of course you didn't." He put a hand on Thomas's shoulder. The airman turned around, nodding his head. "So you heard them?"

Thomas took the charm from where it hung at his neck and let it dangle from his fingertips. He nodded again. "Yeah. I heard it, too," he said. "Palomo, they're okay. They're safe."

"Safe?" Rhys's voice came out a couple octaves higher than usual. He turned to the two librarians who—for their benefit, at least—looked as if they were trying to blend into the wall as they inched away from Palomo. "How do you know they're safe?" he asked in an almost accusatory tone. "They came at us just like Esfani did, with their arms up like they were going to render us unconscious. Again." He ran a hand through his hair. With all the stress he'd been through on the project, he was both surprised as well as lucky that it wasn't coming out in clumps.

"I heard it, boo." Jason put a hand on Rhys's shoulder as his other hand went to the chain hanging at his neck. "They weren't able to say anything like Esfani did, but they still conveyed a message of safety." He looked at Rhys and shook his head. "They're on our side."

Jason's words hung in the air for a moment until he turned. "Wait. Why are you on our side?" he asked the pair. "Why didn't you try and knock us out like Esfani did?" But before they could answer, he held out a finger as if to say, 'one second,' then grabbed Rhys's hand and turned to Palomo. "Take your charm out so you can understand them."

Rhys squeezed Jason's hand.

The pair of librarians, which Rhys now realized must be identical twin sisters, looked at each other before one gestured for the other to speak. "We mean you no harm," the one on the left said, her voice just barely above a whisper.

Whatever she said was in her native tongue, but it even translated in his head barely louder than a murmur. He studied her body language and realized she looked almost meek, for lack of a better word. The speaker looked as if she was shaking, like it had taken all her courage to say anything.

Palomo kept the scalpel gripped tightly at her side as she walked back to the rest of the team, though she never fully turned her back on the librarians. "What do you want from us?"

"We want to help," the second one responded. She looked at the woman next to her; clearly she was the more forceful of the two. "We were in the gallery above when Esfani interviewed your team. She's a brilliant librarian," she said, even as she shook her head.

"But she's…" the first one started, then turned away, also shaking her head. When she finally turned back, she said, "difficult." She looked at the stark white floor tiles, and again whispered, "It is the way of our people, I'm afraid."

"Why would you help us?" Rhys found himself asking. "Why would you not render us unconscious and turn us back over to Esfani?" He knew that his tone was harsh, but after all they had been through, there was very little that he trusted about the Comperians.

"Because you are fascinating creatures," the second one said. She smiled, and Rhys could tell she was trying to be sincere. But still, Rhys found it a little creepy. She turned to Palomo and began to reach out, though Palomo flinched and backed away. At the same time, Palomo put herself in a protective stance between the librarians and the rest of the team. "Sorry," the second librarian continued. "But did you really dream of becoming a ballerina?" Before Palomo could respond, she turned to Jason. "And you. Have you really acted out as a character before an audience? Bringing another artist's words to life?"

"Well, yeah," Jason said. "I mean, not often. But I've danced and acted from time to time." Rhys turned to Jason as his husband cocked his head. "What's so special about that?" After a beat passed, he added, "Wait. I understand how you would know about Palomo, but how do you know about me?" When they didn't answer, he clarified, "That I've acted. On a stage."

Both librarians looked at them with a massive sense of guilt. "I'm sorry," the first one replied. "But when Esfani studied you enough to get the basics of your language, she gleaned a great number of memories from you." She looked at her sister, then back to Jason with a smile. "I am sorry that they were taken from you without your permission. But neither of us have seen someone who has led such a creative life. It seems very freeing."

Jason turned to Rhys. "We introduce these two to Lady Gaga and they'll be set for life."

Rhys couldn't help but laugh, even as it sounded nervous. He caught Palomo rolling her eyes.

The two Comperians turned to each

other, curious looks on their faces, before both nodded. When they turned back, the second one asked, "Do you know what our names are?" As segues went, it was an odd one. Without waiting for an answer, she pointed to herself and said, "Lilji," then looked to her companion and said, "and this is my sister, Lilju."

Rhys and Jason looked at each other like they were missing something. They even chanced a look at Palomo and Thomas, who both stood as if rooted to the spot, looking nonplussed.

When nothing further came, Jason replied, "Those are beautiful names." It sounded more like a question than a statement.

Lilji gave him a small smile, but shook her head as a crestfallen expression covered her face. "They mean first born"—she pointed to herself—"and second born," she added as she pointed to her sister.

"Well, that's…" Rhys started, but his voice trailed off. He looked at Jason, who shrugged. After a second, he added,

"Convenient?"

"Our parents are very much like Esfani," Lilji said. "Actually, most of our population is like her." She crossed her arms over her chest as she shook her head. "This is a wonderful place"—she turned back to face the rest of the building—"full of nearly all of the knowledge in the known universe." When she turned back around, her expression had fallen. "But ours isn't much more than a sterile, clinical life. It leaves a few of us wanting more. So when we learned of your people, we knew there was truly a better life out there." She looked at her sister and smiled. "For people like us."

"What do you mean, 'people like us'?" Thomas asked.

"People who have the experience to truly live."

What Lilji and Lilju went on to describe sounded to Rhys, at least on the surface, like a perfect environment in which to learn. But time after time, Jason had taught him that you could not live on clinical data and research alone, even though it was something Rhys had done throughout college and grad school. When he met Jason, it had opened up the entire world to him, teaching him more about people in one day than Rhys had experienced in the eight years he'd spent getting his Ph.D. Lessons on life were hard for Rhys to learn, none more so than on their trek through Klamath Basin, when Jason had filled in with an intern. Rhys had been content to nerd out with all the data he and his team were gathering, going back to his old habits. But when Jason had decided that Rhys had had enough lab time, he would take him out to nap under a cloud-filled sky or pushed him into the water from their dry, safe space on the dock for an impromptu swim. In a way, it had annoyed him—at first. But when he honestly considered it, he knew Jason was right. What kind of life did he have if he wasn't going to take the chance at living?

"How do we know we can trust you?" Palomo asked. It was then that Rhys realized she had finally stowed the scalpel, probably hidden again in the lining of her boot. He wondered for a moment just how well she would be able to run and not injure herself. Though Palomo was the quietest of the bunch, she was also the craftiest.

Lilji and Lilju exchanged looks, saying things with their eyes that they probably wouldn't be able to convey with words. "A leap of faith," Lilju finally said. She gave them a demure smile. "That's all we can truly offer you. I'm sorry."

"Tell you what," Jason said, "you take us to the rest of our team, and we'll consider that good faith." He gave the women a winsome smile, and they blushed as they smiled back at him.

"Your husband is very charming," Lilji said to Rhys, though her eyes never left Jason.

Rhys dropped Jason's hand in favor of putting an arm around his husband's waist. Jason's ability to charm was a fact that he'd known for almost as long as he'd known Jason. And while he knew he had nothing to worry about, he'd seen both men and women give Jason that look. It stoked something primal in him. "Damn hindbrain," he said, which Jason overheard, then smiled.

Though he couldn't see it, he was sure that Palomo was rolling her eyes. He looked over at her just as she began to speak. "So can you tell us where they're keeping the rest of our team?" She glanced at Rhys and Jason. "The faster we get Captain Franks and the others and get off this planet, the better."

Lilji and Lilju turned to each other. And though again they didn't say anything out loud, their facial expressions changed like they were having an epic conversation.

"I'm sorry," Thomas interrupted, "but are you two actually speaking to one another?" He crossed his arms over his chest and leaned back slightly. "How do we know we can trust you if you're not talking out loud?"

The sisters abruptly stopped and turned to the rest of the team, a bright look of guilt on their faces. "I'm so sorry," Lilji replied. "Nonverbal communication is our normal way of conversing," she said. "It is for most Comperians, only because it is faster and more complete than verbal language." She looked at her sister and put a hand on her arm. "But we will do our best to only speak out loud from here on out."

"No promises if we run into another librarian," Lilju added. Her sister nodded in agreement.

"Let's hope we don't," Palomo replied. "Now where are our people?"

The sisters walked the group through what seemed a labyrinth that twisted back on itself more times than Rhys could keep up with. It took a while for him to notice the patterns of colors and dots at the intersection of two identical hallways for him to understand the way Comperians navigated the building. They mapped it out in logical order, probably with the most efficient use of space available. The Comperians could teach them a thing or two about efficiency. But then again, the Comperians could learn a great deal about human interaction and diplomacy.

Though the hallways they were in previously seemed to bustle with activity, wherever they currently were was mostly quiet. They rounded a corner, where their two companions immediately stopped. When Rhys looked up, he saw why; an elderly librarian stood in the middle of the hallway. She had long, gray hair, some flowing well past her shoulders, but a small ring of hair was wrapped up in a bun almost comically large for such a small-framed woman. The three looked as if they were having a conversation, during which Lilji reached out and patted the older woman's hand as Lilju stood up a little straighter. The elderly woman looked up and considered Rhys and his team for a second. And while he'd never experienced Catholic school, right then he could imagine what it must have been like. Finally, the elderly librarian patted Lilji's arm and began to walk away slowly.

"In here," Lilji said, and waved a hand

over a sensor on the wall. The wall began to move, much like the room that they had been in previously, leading them to a dimly lit room with rows of cots. It looked nearly identical to the room they had been stuck in previously, though this room held more equipment. Lilji urged everyone in and passed her hand over the sensor again, and Rhys watched as the entranceway closed.

He was about to ask where his team was when he saw a distressed look on Lilju's face. "Everything okay?"

But Lilju did not respond to him. Instead, she reached out and put her hands on Lilji's arm. And though she spoke quietly, Lilju's voice sounded like it boomed in the complete absence of sound. "I cannot believe you did that!"

The smile on Lilji's face bloomed brighter. "I honestly did not think I had it within me," she replied. "I think our new friends have already started to improve our lives."

"What did you do?" Rhys asked.

Lilji looked at him as the smile grew even more significant on her face. "I lied."

"Lied?" Jason asked. "What, you mean you've never lied before?"

Rhys considered the librarians' culture for a moment before he realized how monumental it would be. "In a world of nothing but facts and figures, where learning is the number one goal of every person..." He blew out a sigh, pushing his glasses back up the bridge of his nose before he turned to their new friends. "Well, I can see why lying would never come up."

Jason just shook his head. "This place is so weird."

It took a few minutes for them to find the small room where the rest of their team were being held. Though each person was on a cot, just like Rhys and his team had been, there were multiple charms on their heads instead of the single one that Rhys and Jason had experienced. Rhys hurried to Franks's side as the rest of the team fanned out around the others. He studied the contraption wrapped around Franks's head for a second before he looked up. "Why is this one different than the ones they used on us?" he asked as he reached for the device.

"No, no. Don't," Lilji replied as she looked over the device. She ran to a terminal that sat on a small table at the back of the room and punched in a bunch of keys. "It's a full scan."

Rhys shrugged. "Okay? So?"

"If we remove it at the wrong time, it could cause memory loss or other complications." Her expression fell. "Possibly even brain damage."

Thomas, Palomo, and Jason were quickly at Rhys's side. "Okay, so what do we do?" Palomo asked.

Lilji reached out for her sister, who came to her side. "My apologies for this," she said, "but this is the fastest way." She looked Lilju in the eyes, as if studying her sister. But as Rhys watched, the micro-expressions crossing each of their faces told of a tremendous conversation that flowed naturally between them.

"I am sorry," Lilji said once she and her sister had broken their bond, "but I do not know of a way to stop this without harming your team. It is my suggestion that we head back to your planet and return for the others at a date in the future." She held her hands out as if pleading. "I believe it is the only way."

Rhys, Jason, Thomas, and Palomo looked at each other, searching for the right words. No, it wasn't right leaving the rest of their team behind. But if they were caught, they could end up under these scanners themselves—or worse. "What do we do, guys?" he asked.

Before anyone could respond, a thumping sound echoed through the hallway and surrounded them. Both Lilji and Lilju shared a look of panic as Palomo and Thomas took up defensive positions in front of Rhys and Jason. But just as quickly as the sound had started, it began to grow more distant. Whoever was in the hallway wasn't looking for them, or probably even aware that they were just on the other side of the wall. When the final steps faded away, Rhys visibly relaxed and let out a deep breath that he'd held in so long, it made his chest ache.

"Do we really leave them here?" Jason looked to the two airmen for guidance.

Palomo shared a look with Thomas, then stood up a little straighter. "Absolutely not," she replied. "Captain Franks wouldn't leave any of us behind, so there's no way in hell we're leaving her behind."

Palomo's words were comforting. At least they had an answer. But as they contemplated what exactly they could to do both save their friends and avoid capture, a cold feeling of uncertainty settled deep in his gut.

Chapter Sixteen

Getting a schedule for the device was the easiest task that Chaske had accomplished since coming to Sacramento. "It's posted on the freaking internet," he said to the friends that Bartlett had flown in after agreeing to help with the project. Actually, helping wasn't a problem at all. If anything, the sheer number of people willing to step forward and help seemed almost overwhelming. Chaske's was a tight-knit community, and as people began to make plans to fly out, word got around. He had more people offering to help than he knew what to do with.

But more help didn't always mean a better outcome. Because even if just one spoke out of turn, it could jeopardize the entire project.

He and his friends had begun to study the entire process of migration to try and figure out the best way to accomplish their goal. It took a few weeks of gathering information, some from people whose families had migrated, and some from the project's own website. Bartlett showed up quite a few times to ask for status, and he was able to report that he was working on it. It was just that they kept hitting stumbling blocks with whatever plan they came up with.

"But it can't be you, Cuz," one of his friends said. "They're going to be watching you closer than a hawk searching a field for her next meal."

A plan suddenly formed in Chaske's mind. He picked up the phone, called Bartlett, and waited for her to drop by half an hour later.

"So, tell me again how the device works?" he asked.

Bartlett gave him a disdainful look, which he probably deserved. But then again, she had explained how the device worked on several occasions. Still, she went over each step of the process, one by one, from the assembly of the beams to the insertion of the charm. She discussed how the device would stay connected as long as the charm was locked in place, and shut the connection down with a slow, pulsing count of eight. But if for some reason there was something that branched the two worlds, the charm could not be released from the slot, and thus the connection could never be broken. At least, theoretically. There was still no determination on how long the beams held a charge, "Though our scientists on the inside believe that the beam draws its energy from subspace. And since there's an infinite amount of subspace, the connection should theoretically also be infinite."

"Do you have people stationed on Terra yet?" Chaske asked.

Bartlett looked at him with confusion. "Very few," she said. "We have wanted to keep people on this side of the device, for obvious reasons. But we have some assets who have made the journey to Terra and established a base camp two clicks from the device." She looked at him through narrowly slitted eyes. "Why?"

"Would you mind a few more?"

Bartlett studied him for a moment, then

sat back in her chair. "What exactly do you have in mind?"

Chaske sat back into the loveseat and brushed his dark hair away from his eyes. "I believe I have a way to make the machine inoperable and leave the base vulnerable for takeover." He crossed his legs. "Interested?"

Bartlett sat forward, her elbows on her knees. "Tell me more."

*
**

As General Landingham's Jeep carried him from his quarters to the warehouse where the device was stored, he gawped at the sheer size of the line. He knew that they had just surpassed half a million people migrating between the planets, but the sheer number of bodies—both human and livestock—lining the road made it look like their busiest day yet. The line seemed to stretch on for longer than a mile, winding its way through the mouth of the base and starting at a new gate with more security than any ten other bases put together. Each new person wanting to migrate brought with them a number of security issues. As the number of security issues grew, so did the safeguards that Landingham had put into place.

The Jeep finally stopped just short of the doorway, and Landingham got out. He gave the line a final once-over before crossing into the building. "General," one of the airmen said, saluting him as he walked into the makeshift office. It had previously served as a small workspace for a couple of the scientists who had done research on the project before they'd figured out how to turn the damned thing on, much less connect to other worlds. But now, as his office, it was a front-row seat to watch as carriage after carriage of people and goods made the journey across the galaxy. The sight never ceased to fascinate him. Not enough, of course, to make the trip himself, even if just to see how people lived on the other side of the universe. He would one day. Each day he sat in this office was one day closer to retirement and his ability to migrate. He wasn't a young buck anymore, but he knew that all he needed was a cabin somewhere with enough bait for fishing and buckshot for game. That Ingrid had already made the trip to Terra gave him that much more reason to join her.

The folder of threats that greeted him every day again seemed to be much thicker than usual. He picked it up, thumbing through it. "What are we looking at, Daniel?"

"There's been some increased chatter as of late," Airman Daniel Stone said, "which accounts for the extra paperwork this morning. The thing is, General," he said as General Landingham looked up from the paperwork, "most of the chatter is from the Midwest. No reports of it going on out here."

"Still," Landingham said as he went back to the contents of the folder, "better to know about it now than after some event." He turned a few pages, then dropped the folder on the table. A picture slipped out and slowly glided to the floor. "What in blue blazes—"

"And then there's Chaske Oglala, General." Stone picked the picture up, placing it back on top of the folder.

"Why the hell wasn't this at the front of the folder?" Landingham asked brusquely. "We've been watching this man for months." He tapped his finger on the paper as he enunciated each syllable. "This man so much as sets foot within a hundred miles of this base, I want to know about it."

"That's just it, General," the airman continued. "Oglala wants to migrate to Terra."

Landingham stared at him as if the airman had grown another head.

"I know, General," Stone said. "He's been interviewed by a few of our first-liners. Said he can do more if he migrates to Terra to make sure we don't screw up that planet like we've screwed this one up." The airman thumbed at the color-coded tab in the report and turned to it, tapping his fingers on the interview notes.

Landingham could feel his breakfast backing up on him. He looked up at the clock and realized it wasn't even past nine. "I want to talk to him." He got up and went to raid his stash of antacids. "Get his ass in here—now."

"Yes, General." Stone gave a quick salute, then hastily headed out.

As Landingham popped a couple tablets, chewed them, then washed them down with a little bit of water, he sighed. "And it's only Tuesday. Jesus."

Chapter Seventeen

The look on the librarians' faces said that they were at a hopeless crossroads, a puzzle with no solution. If Rhys and the team stayed around much longer, they would surely be caught. But Palomo was right: it wouldn't be right leaving the rest of the team behind. Rhys began to pace the short length of the room, even though he was sure he wasn't equipped to come up with an idea to beat librarians who had been doing this kind of thing for thousands of years.

"Oh!" Lilju turned to her sister. "I have a thought." She gazed at Lilji, no doubt having a quick conversation. Seconds later, she broke the bond and turned to them. "Jason." She reached for him. As he came nearer, she extended her hands. "You have told us about your experiences on the stage, where you take on the role of another person and tell the audience a story."

Jason nodded, then turned to Rhys, his

expression confused. "Yeah," he said, the word more a question than an answer.

Rhys was equally confused as to what she was getting at.

"Have you been in many of these plays? Or anything else that conveys to the audience a strong emotive bond with images and words? Maybe with music?"

"Movies," Jason said.

"Movies?" Rhys asked. "You haven't been in any movies."

"Well, yeah," he replied, "but they don't know that." He stared at Rhys for a second, then gave him a gesture as if he needed to catch up.

"So what, you're going to…" Rhys's voice drifted off as the pieces of the puzzle fell into place. "Oh my god, you're going to replace the memories that they're downloading with movies? How would that even work?" He looked at Jason, then to the twin librarians. "Will it work?"

The sisters had another quick confab before they broke off, and one went to gather additional bits of hardware they needed. "Okay," Lilju said as her sister returned holding something that looked like the charms they were used to, only thicker, "so these are memory cubes. If you can focus on one of these movies, I can pull the information from your memory into and store it on here." She jiggled the memory cubes in her palm. "And then we swap everyone's device out with one of these."

"Will that work?" Rhys asked.

Lilji again turned to Jason. "Are these movies that you talk about as intricate as the plays you've been in?"

"Even more so," Jason replied with a smile. He turned to Rhys. "So we need to pick a movie for each one of these guys that would go with their life. As long as it's not a movie I need to remember from like eight years ago."

Lilji and Lilju shared a curious look, as did Thomas and Palomo. "Why eight years ago?" Thomas asked.

"Because I dragged Rhys to like every movie the first year we met, but... Let's just say

I don't remember the plots to them all that much." Jason smirked at him, then winked at Rhys.

"You two seriously need to get a room," Palomo deadpanned. After a quick roll of her eyes, she asked, "Okay, so what movies?"

"Von Schoor is easy," Jason said. "*An Officer and a Gentleman.*" When everyone focused on him, he shrugged. "What? She's in love with General Landingham."

He was actually right.

"No space movies. No aliens. No apocalyptic endings," Thomas said. "That leaves me out, 'cause that's all I watch."

Rhys closed his eyes and concentrated, trying to come up with a movie that would fit each of their unconscious teammates. When he opened them, Jason's green eyes stared back at him. He first pointed to Franks, and he and Jason said at almost the same time, "*Silence of the Lambs.*"

"Yeah, perfect," Palomo said. "A badass woman with a gun." She smiled at the captain.

Rhys couldn't figure out if the look was admiration or something else.

Jason walked next to the two scientists. "Okay, so *An Officer and a Gentleman* for von Schoor," he said with a smirk. Rhys loved the idea because, even though Ingrid tried to keep it subtle, her admiration for the general was anything but. "And I don't know. Maybe *When Harry Met Sally* for Sheila?" he added as he pointed to Doctor Burnaby.

"She's gonna kill you for that," Palomo replied with a smile on her face.

"Yeah," Jason shot back, "but it's your job to protect me." He winked at the airman, then turned to their companion, whose bulk spilled over the sides of the bed. "What about Luu?"

Rhys came up blank. He had to expand his taste in movies. "Anyone know any good football movies?"

"Oh, *Blind Side*," Thomas said. He turned to Lilju. "Okay, so we've got the movies picked out. Now how do we get them from here"—he pointed to his head—"to there," and pointed to the small cube the librarian held.

Lilju took Thomas by the elbow and sat him down on an empty bed. "Concentrate on a scene from that movie," she said as she brought the device closer to him. "This isn't going to hurt." She put the cube against his forehead.

It took a few seconds, and it looked as if Lilju and Thomas were almost in sync with their facial expressions and breathing. "Okay," Lilju said as she pulled the device back, then pocketed it. "First one down." She looked around, then asked, "Who wants to go next?"

They got all four movies transferred to the memory cubes, and then each person took a spot next to their unconscious teammate. "When I say go," Lilju said, "lift the device from their head and put the memory cube between the three charms. Then lay it down where they won't knock it over. Once it's set, raise them up, then try to get them out of bed." She waited until each person gave her a nod as Lilji worked at a nearby computer terminal.

Rhys took a deep breath, then mentally counted down with her. "One, two, three, go!"

He tried to make it as smooth as possible, but Rhys nearly dropped the memory cube as he took the band from around von Schoor's head. He got the cube and the three charms settled at the head of the bed as he lifted a barely alert, groggy scientist from where she had been laying. "Ingrid? Ingrid, are you okay?" he asked as the others around him stirred. He knelt and looked into the scientist's eyes as he brushed the hair away from her temple. "Are you okay?"

"What the…" was all von Schoor could manage at first. She clutched her head for a second, then shook it. "Thanks," she said as Rhys got her to her feet. It took a few seconds for her to regain her balance, while nearby, Luu wobbled like a newborn foal. But Jason steadied him, and Thomas reached over once he got Franks standing, albeit leaning on the nearby wall.

"Status?" Franks asked. She shook her

head like she was trying to let loose the cobwebs of sleep. It was then that she spotted the twin librarians. "What the hell…"

"They're with us." Rhys kept one arm around von Schoor but held the other one out, hoping she got the message.

"Please," Lilji said as she came to her sister's side, "we mean you no harm."

"It's true, Captain," Palomo said. "They've helped us escape, and came up with a way to get you unhooked from these weird-ass brain wipe thingies."

"We have to come with you after what we've done," Lilju said, her voice quiet. She explained to the captain just how much trouble they would be in if they were caught. "I would not know what the penalty might be. But the last time someone committed the crime of lying, they were jailed and not released until they died." She looked shocked. "His family wasn't even allowed to share in his memories of the experience."

Franks took in the information with an

even keel. "Okay, so if you can help us get off this planet, you can come with us." She looked around as she brushed herself off like she'd been laying in the dirt. "Anyone want to get me caught up?"

Rhys tried to explain all that had happened since they had again been rendered unconscious, after making sure that Esfani hadn't removed the memories of the explosion that could have killed Palomo. He and Palomo then went on to discuss what the airman had found out about the Illeuke, and how the Comperians were systematically slaughtering them. "Honestly, if Esfani would have just admitted that about the Illeuke when we first got here," Rhys said, his voice not quite steady, "we probably would have just turned around and gone back home." The statement was matter-of-fact, but at the same time, it still hurt him to say. After all, there was so much to learn. But part of Rhys realized that there was a moral cost.

"I swear to all that is holy," von Schoor muttered, "I will strangle that woman with my bare hands if I ever see her again."

"Yes, well, we don't want to see her again," Rhys said. "We need to get off this planet as soon as possible."

Franks nodded, then closed her eyes as she brushed her fingertips over her temple. If Rhys was correct, she and the others were probably feeling the after-effects of the devices. He shuddered at the thought of having to entertain a migraine for hours on end on top of being captured. When Franks finally opened her eyes, she added, "Ladies?" as she looked at the librarians. "Suggestions?"

"We've been thinking about that," Lilji said. "First, Lilju and I need to stop by our quarters to grab a few things—"

"You can't bring any clothes or anything," Franks said. Instantly, both sisters' faces fell. "If you're coming with us, I'm sorry to say that nobody can know you're going off-world. Otherwise, you'll blow our cover."

It took a few seconds, but Lilji finally shook her head. "No, no. We can travel with what we have. However, we need to gather a few supplies to make the trip easier for us." When Franks and the team looked at her, she added, "Tools and such. Things that would make travel between planets easier."

Franks slowly nodded her head. "Okay," she finally said. "But nothing that can track you to another planet."

Lilji and Lilju shared a look. "Honestly, these charms, as you call them, perform a great many tasks, and one of them is indeed tracking. So it is without a doubt that we may be tracked from planet to planet as long as we have them. Any of us."

Franks smirked and shook her head. "Charming," she said, and then almost immediately held up a hand. "Pun not intended." After another sigh, she pointed to the librarians. "You two, go get your things," and gestured toward the hallway. "Meanwhile, we know our weaponry is outside the building. And if we show up, we'll no doubt be caught. So in the meantime"—she lifted her arms as if to encompass the entire room—"spread out and see what you can find."

"Oh," Rhys said as Airman Palomo reached down and took the blade from her boot, "yes, there is that."

Captain Franks smiled as the surgical instrument gleamed in the dimmed light of the room. "Atta girl."

*
**

They hadn't found much that would have made for easy weapons by the time the librarians returned. Not to say a couple of metal legs that made up part of the frame of one of the beds couldn't do some damage. But they were a lot more primitive than a gun or grenade would ever be.

"Captain?" Lilji said as she and her sister came back into the room. "We think we have come up with a plan to get out of here with the fewest interactions with our fellow librarians." She went on to describe the area where she and Lilju shared a small lab a few floors below where they currently were. "The corridors to get there are long, but at this time of day, there should be very few people around. It is mealtime, and most people will either be at home with their families or out in the market square getting foodstuffs."

"But the Cludiant is just off the market square," Rhys replied. "How are we supposed to get out there?"

"Actually, if we can time it right, we can walk out when there are the fewest people around and make it look like we are walking you back to the device," Lilji said. "It is usually done with much more senior librarians, but I think we, as you might say, can 'pull it off.'" She smiled.

"What is that?" Jason asked. It was then that Rhys realized that Lilju wore a small brown bag on a long, leathery piece of thin fabric around her neck.

Lilju patted the small bag at her neck. "These are the items we need to forge new charms that can get us between planets." Her fingers danced gently over the tanned fabric.

Rhys wondered morosely if the fabric was made from Illeuke skin, though it seemed more like elk or deer. "And you know how to make a charm that connects two different planets? Ones that we don't have charms for already?"

Lilju smiled. "It is one of the first things you are taught as a librarian, yes," she said. "Not the construction of the charms themselves, but rather the way that the devices on each planet operate and connect to one another."

"Yeah, well, hopefully we won't need it." Franks looked around the room. "We ready?"

Each person gave their response. And within moments, they were ready to take the chance and finally get off this planet.

They fell in line behind the twin librarians and walked the sterile corridors of the building until they reached the small lab Lilji and Lilju used to do research. Rhys could immediately tell that this workspace was different than the others they had been in; though it remained almost as spartan as every other part of the building they had seen, there were still the occasional touches of personality here and there. It spoke volumes of their guides' yearning. Unlike the sterile, solid-color backgrounds on the computer terminals, the twin monitors displayed image after image of other planets—pictures that showed the dark green of a rainforest, broken up in the middle by a pair of beautiful, colorful birds. That picture dissolved, replaced by a dark gray image of the side of a volcano, a small vent opened on the side with molten lava oozing out, the bright orange of fire in the middle with the edges darkened as the lava flowed.

"Are these places you have studied?" Rhys couldn't help but ask of the librarians as they locked up the offices and picked up a few more items to tuck into their robes.

Lilji smiled as she nodded. She held out her hand and urged, "Each of you need to take a pair." The small, eraser-shaped objects were pink and mostly pliable in his hand as Rhys rubbed one between his fingers.

"What is it?" he asked.

"These will protect you from the somnumtus, should we be discovered by another librarian." She looked at her sister, both aware that the word had not translated. "When Esfani raised her hands, opened her mouth, and uttered the sound that caused you to pass out," Lilji replied. "When we swore off weapons hundreds of years ago, our scientists learned what we could about defensive weaponry that we could use just generated from our own corporeal being."

"Makes sense," Rhys said.

"Gimme a SIG Sauer any day," Palomo said as she put one of the plugs in.

"Only one," Lilji said as she held up one of the earplugs. "We need to move together until we get outside. Once we are out of the library and headed for the device, you'll want to slip the other one in."

"What if we get caught before then?" Rhys asked.

Lilji and Lilju shared a look. "If we are caught before we make it outside, we will have bigger issues to deal with than these." She had a sour look on her face, which Rhys completely understood. For all intents and purposes, the sisters were committing treason against their own people. If caught, they would be dealt with swiftly and efficiently. He tried not to think about what might happen to him and his team.

After Rhys slipped one of the earplugs in, he experienced two different feelings that each gave him a shudder. First, the feel of the material against his skin was not unlike the lightly-furred skin he previously felt when they passed the Illeuke soon after they had gotten to the planet. Second—and much more unsettling—was the fact that once he had placed the plug into his ear, he felt it not just mold to the unique shape of his ear, but reach in farther as if the device automatically burrowed deep into the ear canal to enable blocking of all sounds.

"Yeah." Jason pocketed the second earplug, then took Rhys's hand into his own. "Not unlike a tick trying to burrow into your skin, huh, boo?"

Rhys couldn't help but stop mid-step and give in to the whole-body shake as the sensation Jason had just described overtook him. Sure, Rhys loved the outdoors; it was part of being a good biologist. But ticks and other leech-like insects were a part of the job nobody ever told him about, and something he detested. He just didn't want to deal with the thought.

Lilji got them underway, and Rhys was glad that he held Jason's hand; predictably, the blockage in Jason's ear sent his already terrible balance into a tailspin. He stumbled over his own feet a few times as they once again walked through the sterile corridors of the building. "You okay?" Rhys asked as the twins stopped them at a glass wall.

When Jason didn't answer, Rhys squeezed his hand.

"Huh?" He looked at Rhys, then pointed at the ear he'd stuffed the earplug into; he and Rhys had both put them into their right ear. So Rhys stepped to the left, then held Jason's other hand. Even though he would have some trouble hearing Jason, at least Jason would be able to listen to him unencumbered.

"Okay, just out these doors is the marketplace," Lilji said. Rhys watched as she looked around, everyone acknowledging her. "We're going to cut through the marketplace and then walk toward the device like we are part of the delegation that walks teams away from the library. By that time we should be able to escape with no problem." She looked pointedly at Palomo and motioned her to come closer.

Palomo did so. "Yes?"

"I need you at the front. You are the keymaster, as Jason has called you. Is that correct?" When Palomo nodded, Lilji said, "Good. Keep up with me, and Lilju will escort the rest. We will need to connect with your planet as soon as we reach the device."

As soon as Palomo nodded, the glass entryway began to splay open, and Lilji and Palomo quickly made their way out of the building. "Quickly, quickly," Lilju said, her voice barely above a whisper as they picked up the pace and continued following. But Rhys watched as Lilju's attention divided from where they were going to where they had just come from. A worried look spread across her face as she glanced back.

"Everything okay?" he asked.

Lilju offered him the smallest of smiles. "Well, we have not been attacked by the library's automated defenses," she said as she glanced back. "So that is good."

They continued hurriedly through the marketplace with very few librarians around, and those who were seemed to pay more attention to the food stalls than the group of people hurrying to the Cludiant. But while there were very few librarians around, there were countless Illeuke at every turn. Most mindlessly restocked items, while others careened around the marketplace on unknown missions, either for themselves or—more likely—for a librarian. Rhys almost tripped over a couple of them, though their twin prehensile tails were quite useful when it came to clumsy humans. The Illeuke managed to get Rhys righted before he was even aware that he was about to fall. Jason, on the other hand, face-planted into a table of soft fruit.

"I'm okay, I'm okay," he said as a couple of Illeuke descended upon the table to clean up the mess, and one of them held out a cloth for him to clean up with. "Thanks, little dude." He wiped the dust and fruit detritus from his face, then handed back the cloth.

"Come, come." Lilju took one of Jason's hands into her own. And if Rhys's and Lilju's help weren't enough, Luu came up behind Jason and put a hand on his shoulder.

"You want I should carry you, boss?" Luu teased with a wink.

Jason smiled in response. "Just don't make Rhys jealous," he replied. "He may not have as many muscles as you, but he's scrappy."

If Rhys hadn't already been short of breath from running, he would have laughed.

They got to the corridor where the device was stationed and turned the corner just in time for Rhys to watch as Palomo took the charm connecting Comperian to Terra from her wrist glove. She slipped the device inside, and Rhys held his breath, ready for the journey back home and away from this crazy planet. But instead of the familiar smell of ozone and the bright, sunny day of Terra, Palomo instead looked up at the rest of the team, her expression filled with fear.

"It won't seat." She pulled the charm from the device. She held it out, urging Rhys to take it from her. "It's normally drop, seat, click. But right now all I can get it to do is drop it into the slot. It will not seat, so I can't click it into place."

Rhys took the cooled charm into his hand and ignored the pulling sensation that usually overwhelmed him whenever he held a charm this close to the Cludiant. He and Jason knelt, and each of them took a go at trying to get the pendant to click into place, with no luck.

"Uh, Captain?" Rhys held the charm in his outstretched hand. "What do we do now?"

Captain Franks considered the situation. "They must be mid-transport of another group of settlers." She nodded at Rhys. "Can you tell how much time we have until this transport sequence is completed?"

Rhys looked at the custom watch that fit snug at his wrist. "Last I remember it was six-hour connections every eight-hour period, starting at 4 A.M., Tambra."

Rhys kept staring at his watch. It was just past 9 P.M. in Sacramento, which meant if they were following the schedule, the connection still had a few hours to go. He shook his head, knowing he couldn't hide the dejected look on his face. "Another five hours to go, Captain."

"Shit, shit, shit," Franks replied. The Comperian sun was directly overhead, and the heat felt closer to Terra's than when they had first arrived on the planet many hours before. "Suggestions?" she asked, brushing the sweat from her brow. "Any place we can hide and wait this out?" she asked Lilji and Lilju.

Both Lilji and Lilju's faces suddenly were overtaken with alarm. "Oh my," Lilji replied. She looked at her sister, and the concern grew. "They know we have escaped," she said to Franks, but continued to look at her sister. "A planet-wide notification just went out to all Comperians." She turned to Franks as she reached out and grasped the Captain's arm. "They will be looking for us," she said, "and they will use the Illeuke—" Her face went pale, her eyes wide in panic. "She's coming!"

In the momentary chaos, it seemed as if everyone's voices rose at once, even as the Illeuke continued to move around the area, stacking their wares. Lilji and Lilju shared a quick conversation—or at least, that was what it looked like to Rhys—as their wide, panicked-looking eyes glanced at each other, then around. "Come, come," Lilji said, then rushed them over to one of the nearby tables, stacked high with food. Well, it looked like food to Rhys. First there was something that looked like elongated asparagus in neat stacks, surrounded by what looked like a purple softball, the flesh dimpled like a grapefruit. At the ends of both tables were brown balls with several darkened spots that, were this Earth, Rhys would swear they were coconuts.

There was a disturbance as something glided low to the ground, approaching at a rapid pace. Rhys held out his second earplug, but Lilji shook her head, so he held it tight.

As Esfani approached, Lilju smiled, and with a gesture, turned everyone's attention to the table. "And these," she said as she picked up the coconut-looking item, "are what we call grimtala. They have a sweet, sweet juice inside, and a delicious pink flesh that is very nutritious." She turned as Esfani stepped off some sort of small flying platform. "Ah, Esfani," she said with a smile. "How wonderful of you to join us."

Esfani glared at the sisters, then turned to glare at Rhys and his team. She opened her mouth, but before she could utter a sound, Lilji reached out and grabbed her arm. Not only did it distract Esfani, but the action resulted in the librarian turning her heated ire on the sister.

"Esfani, please," Lilju said, her voice breaking. She suddenly returned to a timid state, reminding Rhys of how she'd been when they first met.

"We were just taking them for food," Lilji said. But at the same time as she spoke, Lilji's voice whispered in Rhys's head. And judging by the sudden movement by others on the team, theirs as well. *She cannot render you unconscious again,* Lilji's voice rang out. *Sister and I are protecting you.*

"Yes," Lilju said, a simple smile quickly covering her face. "We have not been that hospitable to our guests, and we thought we might show them some of our favorite foods." She picked up the coconut-like fruit. "These are my favorite," she said, then turned to Esfani.

"What about you?"

Esfani's expression grew dark, her eyes closing to slits. She turned to Lilju, then Lilji. "I will deal with you two later," she said, her voice low. "Now take them back to their cells."

"May we get something for them to eat first?" Lilji asked.

Again, Esfani's expression went dark. She opened her mouth and began to raise a hand, and even though Rhys knew they were protected, he couldn't help but flinch.

But before the eerie sound could fall from her lips, Lilju swung the grimtala at Esfani's head. It cracked with a sickening thud against her skull, Esfani's long, dark hair quickly untangling from the neat bun it had been put up in. Esfani's eyes rolled back, and she fell to the dusty ground as pink liquid dripped from a crack in the fruit.

"*Sister!*" Lilji cried out, though her lips were parted in a surprised smile.

Lilju dropped the fruit, where it was quickly picked up and re-stacked by an Illeuke.

She reached out and put a hand on the being, then said, "Medical." The creature was quickly joined by two others, and Esfani's limp body was rushed away.

"What?" Lilju finally asked, a newfound sense of authority in her voice. "I simply cannot allow people like *her* to harm our friends." They all turned to watch Esfani's unconscious body as it neared the building. "But also," she started, shrinking into herself slightly, "when they revive her, we will *not* escape a second time." She turned to Rhys and Jason. "We must leave."

There was still too much time to pass before Earth disconnected from Terra. Franks looked around. "Suggestions?" She asked the team. "Anyone?"

The airmen all looked ready to fight, while the scientists and Jason seemed extremely worried. Rhys had no idea what their future might be if they were again captured by Esfani, but he was pretty sure that it would mean Lilji and Lilju would be imprisoned for life—or worse.

Lilju reached for the bag around her neck and pulled out a couple different charms. They each had a distinct set of markings on them, though a few seemed to be blank, at least from what Rhys could tell. She said something to Lilji that did not translate, and after a beat, Lilji nodded her head.

As Lilju slipped the charm into the device, Rhys took a tiny bit of comfort from the click of the pendant locking into place, followed by the quick smell of ozone. But when the connection stabilized, there was no scenery. Before them, just beyond the blue-tinted event horizon, lay nothing but darkness.

"The device on this planet we call 'Limbo' is hidden," Lilji explained. "It is a safe planet. We believe their civilization died off many, many years ago due to toxins in their environment. Lilju and I have gone here several times to explore over the years. There are some predators, though we have crafted some weapons and keep them on the other side."

"Why Limbo?" Rhys asked. "And why

is it so dark?"

"The planet is between civilizations at the moment, so the name seemed to fit. The people that were here, for whatever reason, stored their device in a cave. We are not sure why, but once we get to the other side, we should be able to gather our weapons and stay there until we can make it back to your planet."

A scuffle sounded, and voices called out from the marketplace. The librarians must surely know that they were trying to head back, and from the sounds of it, were ready to stop them.

"No time to waste," Franks said. "Everyone through the device." When no one moved, she shouted, "Now!"

That gave them the impetus to start moving, and before Rhys knew it, Jason was pulling him through the Cludiant. It began with the familiar feeling of tugging as he stuck one leg into the device, his lower leg crossing the event horizon and settling onto solid ground somewhere else in the universe. He closed his eyes and took another step, and before he knew it, stood on solid ground in the cave of this limbo planet.

They stood silently for a moment before Jason pulled him farther into the cave, which was farther than the light from Comperian could reach. He was hesitant to move deeper into the blackness, but had to because of the size of their team. He turned back as the last of the team came through the device, and Franks leaned down and pulled the charm from where it was locked in the slot. He watched her take one final look around, then stepped through the device, the slow pulse of the beams providing the barest hint of light for a count of eight, and then as the connection between the planets was severed, left them in complete darkness.

Chapter Eighteen

Though ten of them stood in what must have been a massive cave—a strong airflow surrounded them, as well as a generous echo that followed each sound—Rhys still felt the claws of claustrophobia dig into his skin. At least the cave was cool; the distant sound of dripping water reminded him of chilly, wet mornings in Portland. He refused to let himself panic, but at the same time, pulled Jason closer to him for what little comfort he could take. He could still only hear out of one ear, though besides the dripping water, all he could hear were his teammates' footfalls. After a second, he pulled the earplug from his right ear and tucked it into a pocket, along with the second. "God, I hate this," he said against Jason's cheek.

Not a second later, a green light cut through the darkness, just bright enough for Rhys to see the bewildered expressions of the others around him, as well as the walls of the cave half a dozen feet away. He turned and saw Luu, who towered over the rest of the group, holding what was essentially an industrial-sized glowstick above his head.

"Thanks, Hien," Franks said. "First, Lilji and Lilju," she said to get the librarians' attention, "is there any danger of them knowing what planet we've escaped to?"

"No," Lilji responded. "Though we have gained a great deal of knowledge about the devices, we still do not have a way to track what planet was accessed last."

"Good." Franks walked up to where Lilji and Palomo stood, cracking her own glowstick. "Then let's try to get out of here and into some sunshine where we can at least see each other."

"This way." Lilji led them through the maze of the darkened cave, the green light of Franks's glowstick illuminating their way. It was probably only fifty or sixty feet from where the device had been stored to the mouth of the cave, the growing light from the outside announcing their progress. And while they were amid daylight, there was no sunshine to be found. Instead, the mouth of the cave revealed that they were in the middle of what Rhys considered an "East Coast downpour." Portland rain was unique in that it was more often a gentle drizzle that lasted for hours on end. But what they were experiencing on this planet was a torrential downpour, one that spurred flooding for miles around. He'd been through many rainstorms like this during his time in college back east.

"Great," Franks said as they huddled at the mouth of the cave. "Well, it doesn't look like we're going to be able to leave the cave unless we plan on getting soaked." Rhys and Jason were used to it, but he knew traveling while you were uncomfortable in your own clothes was something not everyone was used to.

Rhys tried to force a change in perspective. "So guys"—he put a hand on Lilju's arm—"how do we get home? What do we have to do to forge a new charm to connect this planet with ours?"

"Yeah, how does that thing dial, anyway?" Jason pointed back into the cave. "I mean, it has to be some sort of mapping software, or telemetry or..." He looked at Rhys. "I got nothin'," he finished with a shrug.

Lilju pulled the small satchel from around her neck and carefully opened it. She removed a charm and held it out for Rhys. "It's quite simple," she said. "Each side of the device is coded with a special tool to indicate the catalog number of that planet. You put the catalog number on each side, and the device knows to connect those two addresses."

"That's it?" Jason asked. "Two different catalog numbers and boom, you're able to connect two planets?" He looked at Rhys, then shook his head. "What's the catch?"

"How do you know the catalog number?" Rhys figured that was the critical question.

Lilji smiled. "It's actually one of the first things you learn when you enter the library.

As our teacher said, you have to learn the past to shape the future. And the catalog numbers of the planets are a rich, important past that you must know before you are allowed to manufacture your first charm. So you must memorize the catalog first, and then the process builds from there."

"That doesn't sound too hard," Doctor Burnaby said. "And it's like any other science you undertake—learn the basics, then build onto that."

"How many planets do you have cataloged?" Rhys asked.

"As of our last visit—the one before your planet—41,267."

The sheer number boggled Rhys's mind. "And you have to memorize them? All of them?" He could barely remember his teacher's name from first grade, and the Comperian librarians had not just to learn, but memorize them for later on? It completely threw him for a loop.

"Indeed," Lilju replied. "But it's better

than having to memorize every planet with a Cludiant on it, as you call them."

Rhys and Jason shared a curious look, and Rhys wasn't sure he wanted to know exactly how many planets that consisted of.

"Nearly half a million," Lilju said in answer to the unasked question. "Even though most of the inhabited planets in the solar system have a device on them, many of them are either inhabited by people who either do not know of, or cannot use the device. Or they are like the people of this planet." She gestured out the mouth of the cave, and in what looked to be afternoon sunlight, Rhys saw buildings in the distance. Or at least what were once buildings, now left to decay. "These people died many, many thousands of years ago," she said, her tone quite matter-of-fact.

"Died?" von Schoor asked, her voice popping up from the back of the group. She pushed her way forward as she put her hand over her mouth. "Was it some sort of plague? Something we need to worry about?"

"Oh, do not worry, Doctor." Lilju plastered a smile on her face. "These people died out as a result of natural phenomenon. They built their civilization near what you would call a super volcano so that they could harness it for energy. But when the volcano came back to life after thousands of years of dormancy, the gas it released killed the majority of the population. The rest died out within a year due to starvation and disease."

The smile on Lilju's face was disconcerting. It somehow reminded Rhys of a bubbly newscaster back on Earth who could announce that two jumbo jets had collided, killing hundreds of people, without once letting their smile falter.

"So that's it," Rhys said. "You recall the catalog number of this planet and our home planet, mark it somehow on the blank charm you have, and then, boom—we're home free?" When both Lilji and Lilju smiled and nodded, Rhys said, "It sounds too easy. There's got to be a catch."

"Well, it does have to be done by fire," Lilji said. "Does that make it sound difficult enough for you?"

Rhys nodded. "Yeah," he said. "That'll do."

Franks immediately took over as she moved to the front of the group and stood out in the rain, which still hadn't let up. "If we need fire, we're not going to get it in here without killing ourselves with toxic fumes in the process." She turned around, and the group surveyed the area. "Over there." She pointed the direction of the setting sun. "Looks like there's a few little buildings less than two clicks." She turned back and considered the rest of the group. "Everyone here up for a little walk?"

The question was more for the civilians, who all nodded. Rhys knew that the airmen would consider whatever Franks said an order. "Then let's move out." Franks took the lead and started for the remains of what looked like a small settlement.

Torrential rain slowed what would have

usually been a half-hour walk, at the very most. But Franks marched on, turning to check on the rest of the group when there was a yelp or some other disturbance. More than once, von Schoor managed to get caught up in some blackberry-type brambles. And though the librarians were soaked, their multi-colored robes covered in mud, the expressions on their faces were more akin to kids being allowed to play out in the rain for the first time in their lives.

"This is so exciting!" Lilju said as the group took turns hopping over a small creek that had jumped its banks from the downpour. It was barely two feet across, and everyone on the team had appropriate footwear. That is, except for the librarians, who wore meager sandals that did nothing to keep out the rain and mud.

"I take it you don't get out much?" Rhys asked. "This is close to what, in my profession, we would call 'fieldwork.'"

"So you've done this type of hiking before?" Lilji asked. When both Rhys and Jason nodded, she added, "All our lives, every learning situation we have come across has been within the confines of the library. That is why Lilju and I love coming to this planet."

"Why is that?" Jason asked.

Rhys looked over when he noticed Doctor Burnaby edging closer, paying attention to the conversation. He smiled at her, but she failed to notice, too focused on what the librarian was saying.

"This is not a civilization we could interact with, because the last remaining souls died out many, many eons ago. And while Esfani and the librarian elders maintain that we learn from other civilizations when they come through the device to our home world, Lilju and I have come here on many occasions, just to observe." When both Rhys and Doctor Burnaby gave her a curious look, she added, "Not too far from the mouth of the cave, mind you," she said as she pointed to where they had come from. "But it is still more than we have ever done for the library."

Rhys wondered what it would have been

like growing up in such a sheltered, restrictive civilization. The part of him that loved knowledge and learning yearned for that type of structure. But the part of him that kept him outdoors—what had inspired him to become a biologist in the first place—was what kept him going. He couldn't imagine having one without the other. But as his mind contemplated, he went back to something Lilji had said. "Wait a second. So you're saying your fellow librarians don't go off-world?"

Lilji shook her head as she stepped across another puddle, her sandals squishing in the mud. "Not in many, many years," she replied. "Librarians believe we can learn from people who come through the device. And when the device stands quiet, we have much that we can learn just from each other, from biology to anatomy. We are always working on something."

Rhys nodded. The more he learned about the Comperians, the more pity he felt toward them, tinged with a dark shade of disgust.

"It's just around this bend," Franks called from the front of the line. Rhys chanced a look at where Franks was rounding and saw that the trail thinned from the leisurely path they'd been on to one that was barely wide enough for one person between the jutted rocks and overhangs. He and Jason could no longer walk hand in hand, so he dropped Jason's hand, but made sure he was okay traipsing in the mud by himself. Farther down the path, all he saw was mud and rain. And was that a trace of sulfur on the air?

"Captain?" Rhys hurried his pace, and he rounded the sharp corner just as Franks urgently called back, "Whoa, whoa, everyone!" He pushed past the two librarians, Jason hot on his heels, until he stood next to Captain Franks.

"What is it?" he asked, though his eyes were on their surroundings, not Franks. "Whoa."

Not that he needed to wait for Franks's assessment. About ten feet beyond Franks was an arcing jet of lava that spewed from some underground cauldron. The lava itself did not seem like it posed that great a danger to the group, though the steam caused by the torrential rain landing on the fresh magma raised the temperature a dozen degrees, as well as obscuring their view. A breeze pushed through, and that was when he saw it. Just beyond the spewing magma was the land bridge that connected them with the utility-like buildings only another hundred or so feet away. But to call it a land bridge was being generous. The land seemed to fall away, revealing an ancient riverbed fifty feet below. What little he could see of it, that was. The lava flowed into part of the riverbed and caused steam to rise, which explained the erratic wind patterns they had experienced after crossing the bend. The area had been a land bridge at some point in the past, but had been eroded by time and the never-ending flow of water. Rhys studied it for a moment, then turned to Franks. "Is it passable?"

He studied the sight as Franks began to nod. "It looks like it."

She gestured for Rhys and Jason to turn back with her. "Luu, Thomas," she said to the two airmen who brought up the rear, "on the way down here, were you able to spot any other passable areas?"

"No, Captain," Luu replied. "We came down what looks like the only safe way, although there's no telling what's on the other side of the mountain."

Von Schoor sneezed, and Rhys was reminded that they were soaked and in need of shelter.

"And we need to get the civilians out of this weather." After considering it a second, Franks patted Luu on the back. "You're with me," she said, and then pushed their way to the front of the line. Rhys stayed close behind them both.

"Oh, snap," Luu said as soon as the two angled around the ledge, giving them the best view of the path forward. "This'll be something."

"You're the egghead structural

engineer." Franks bobbed her head toward their destiny. "What do you think?"

At that moment, Rhys wished he had more of a structural engineering background instead of his biology degree. But then again, without his degree—and without Jason in his life—they wouldn't be anywhere near here. Wherever *here* was.

"There's only five steps total," Luu said. "And the whole chasm isn't more than twelve feet wide. They look like they can hold probably three hundred pounds each, maybe four? That third one might sway a little because of the thinner base. But if these things have been able to stand the updraft of all that steam, it should be fine."

Franks nodded as she considered the airman's words.

"I'll go first, Captain," Luu said as a gust of wind made Rhys pull back slightly. "If it can hold me, then it can hold the rest—" He stopped and looked around, suddenly waggling his foot like an unseen ferret had clamped onto a toe. "Hot! Hot! Hot! Hot!" he chanted, turned, then charged up the path to a small puddle of water, into which he dunked his now steaming boot. After a second, he let out a sigh. "Oh, thank god."

"Hien?" Rhys ran over to where the airman stood, Captain Franks at his side a second later. "What's going on?"

Airman Luu pulled his now soggy boot out of the puddle and displayed it for the rest of the team. Off-balance, he leaned on Rhys—who felt like the airman could crush him with the smallest effort—as he held his boot out. It took a second, but Rhys finally spotted it. Part of the airman's boot along the ankle had melted. It hadn't gotten to the skin, but Rhys knew that the steel-reinforced boots had to have gotten quite uncomfortable rather quickly, with the errant lava that had dropped onto Hien's ankle heating it far past painful.

"You okay, Airman?" Franks asked.

Luu nodded, then let go of Rhys and stood on his own. "Yes, ma'am," he finally replied as he wiped the sweat from his brow.

"You still feel like being a guinea pig?" She nodded back to the waiting bridge.

With a grunt, Luu nodded and walked back to where he and Franks had been standing just moments before. He waited for a second, looked back with a nod, then turned and stepped out onto the first pillar. Then the second. Third. Fourth. Fifth. And with a final step, he landed on solid ground on the other side. "Rock solid," he yelled across the cavernous yawn. "They were really stable," he called across. "No wobbling."

"Good," Franks replied. "Palomo, you go next in case Luu needs help with anything. Scientists next, then Rhys and Jason. Then the librarians, and then finally me and Thomas." Rhys nodded, as did the rest of the team, so Franks gestured to the stones and ordered, "Be careful of wind gusts. They can set you off balance or throw lava your way." Rhys saw Burnaby and von Schoor share a worried look, though Franks missed it.

"Just think of it as fieldwork, Doctors,"

he said with a wink.

"Move out!"

Rhys was glad that Jason had gotten him used to regular hikes around Oregon. Sure, some hiking had been part of Rhys's job, but Jason had introduced hiking as the cure for too-quiet weekends. There was barely any corner of the Pacific Northwest they hadn't explored in the eight years they'd been together, though he had to admit that besides the rain, their current surroundings weren't like any hiking adventure they'd experienced.

Jason walked in front of him and stumbled slightly as he approached the stepping-off point for the first pillar.

Rhys automatically set a steadying hand on Jason's shoulder. "Be careful, Jase!"

"I'll be fine." Jason glanced back, and there was something worrisome hidden in his expression that Rhys didn't want to see.

"I'm right behind you." And even though he was inches away from his husband, he still worried.

Behind Rhys, Lilji said, "I cannot believe we are finally doing something worthy of an adventure!" He was about to turn when a blob of glowing lava, aided by a gust of wind, fell from the sky, which separated him and Jason. As he leaned out of the projectile's way, he bumped into Lilji. "Sorry, sorry." He would be the one to stumble after telling Jason to be careful.

"Oh, ow!" came a startled cry from behind him. When he turned, he realized that there had been another small wind-blown patch of lava, but this one had landed on the fabric of Lilji's flowing robes. Before he could do anything, Lilju was at her sister's side, brushing out the small embers that the lava had ignited. Lilji's robes had been singed, but she was unharmed.

"Let's not lose our heads before we cross the bridge, shall we?" Lilju said with a smirk. She held the fabric out, letting the rainstorm soak the cloth, dousing any ember that remained.

Lilji nodded, then fanned herself with a hand. Even though the temperatures were on the cooler side, because of the change in the wind, steam was blowing about and everything was growing warmer. "May I have some water?" Lilji asked.

Thomas took a canteen from his belt and held it out for her, which she drank from greedily. "We'll need to re-up our supplies once we're settled in," he said as Lilji handed him the mostly-drained canteen.

"Come along, sister," Lilju said. She gestured for Rhys to go ahead.

Rhys glanced back and saw that the two librarians were close behind, and turned back to make sure Jason had made it safely to the other side.

The first step onto the stone pillars was slightly nerve-wracking. Rhys tried to focus on each stone foothold instead of the bubbling cauldron of steam stirring fifty feet below them, but he was suddenly in his head. The moment you tell yourself not to think about something, that's the only thing that your mind can process. He paused and took a breath, then took another step, even as his mind circled on the sensation of falling and the morbid thoughts of what would happen to a human body if it landed on a pile of rocks versus a body of water. And could a human even survive if the water was deep enough? Surely not. But then again, he was a biologist, not a pathologist. Biology gave him the chance to study life, and he tried to focus on that. Life. Living.

"C'mon, boo," Jason called from the other side.

When Rhys opened his eyes, he realized that he had paused much longer than he'd realized. He took a step onto the third stone and let out a breath, then onto the fourth.

Behind him was the sound of a scuffle, and Rhys stopped moving and turned where he saw Lilju's arms windmilling. She had maybe stepped on her robes, or maybe lost a sandal. He couldn't imagine trying to cross these in a pair of sandals. The sooner that they got back to Terra and got the sisters set up with some real clothes and shoes, suitable for environments like this, the better. "Are you okay?" he asked as Lilju finally stilled.

Somewhere far below, a sound echoed off the rocks as the vapors swirled endlessly.

"I lost a sandal," Lilju replied. "Sister?" She craned her head around slightly. "Be careful. This isn't the most hospitable environment for us."

The look on Franks's face was beyond worried. "Just take it slow," she said to them, her voice calm and soothing. "We've got all day."

Rhys turned back and walked the fourth and fifth steps, then stepped onto solid ground. "C'mon, Lilju."

Lilju squirmed for a second, and Rhys watched as her second sandal got pushed over the edge of the stone. It landed with a flop dozens of feet below, probably nearby the other one. She took a breath, nodded, and again got underway.

"Sister?" Lilji asked.

Lilju was mid-step between the third and fourth stepping stones when she turned back. With her attention divided, she misstepped onto the fourth stone. And because of the weather, her feet didn't gain purchase on the rain-slicked surface. In an instant, she landed stomach-first on the fourth stone, knocking the wind out of her. And though Lilju and her sister were small in build and stature, her fall made the entire pillar sway gently.

"Stop! Everybody stop!" Franks called, even as Lilji cried out for her sister.

"Oh my god," Rhys said as Jason grabbed his arm. He held Jason back from returning to the pillars, sure that Jason would risk his life trying to save her.

"Lilji! Lilji!" Franks called. When she turned, Franks ordered, "Carefully turn around and come back. I need to get out there and help her."

"Let me do it." Thomas started unloading his gear, dropping it where he stood.

"Let me, Captain."

"No," Luu called back, which caused everyone to look up. "That one is the weakest of all the pillars. It wouldn't hold you both. And if you tried to pull her up, you'd knock it down."

"I'll go," Palomo said next to him. "I can do it." She took off the gear she was carrying. "Let me, Captain."

The sound of Lilju's sobs shattered Rhys's heart. "It's gonna be okay," he said, even as worry ratcheted within him. "We're gonna get you off there."

"No," Lilju said through a sniffle. "It's the sachet."

"The what?"

Rhys followed Lilju's finger to where the sachet had been hanging around her neck. Only now it was no longer around her neck, but sat a few feet below her, just out of arm's reach. "It came off when I fell." She reached for it, struggling to inch closer, though the wind whipped the tanned hide rope just out of reach. She leaned forward and inched herself closer, but it was no use. The sachet could have been a hundred miles away, for all her work.

Lilju looked up, then nodded. She scooted backward, away from the sachet until her small frame was hanging off the back of the stepping stone.

"What are you doing?" Franks called. "Stop!" When the librarian refused, Franks again said, "Lilju, I need you to stop what you're doing. We are trained for this kind of thing. We can get it. I need you to get back to your feet and walk to the other side."

"It's my responsibility, Captain Franks," she replied.

"Your responsibility is to be here with your sister," Franks called back. Rhys looked over and saw Lilji staring at the scene with a petrified look. "Lilju, listen to me." Franks's voice quieted. "Please."

Lilju wrapped her legs around the pillar as best she could. She scooted down, careful of keeping herself away from where the sachet perilously hung. She moved around the pillar slowly, grasping so tight that her hands went white with the strain.

"About two more inches, Lilju," he heard himself saying, unsure where the calm in his voice came from. "You can do it."

Those two inches took what seemed like six hours. But she finally let go of one side of the pillar long enough to grasp the sachet between her fingers.

Rhys let out a breath he hadn't realized he'd been holding.

Lilju pulled the sachet back and put it between her teeth as she slowly started to inch upward. Though she was tiny, she could move better than he figured she might. Especially for someone who had never left the comfort of her home and lab back on Comperian.

When she was close enough, Lilju reached up, took the sachet from between her teeth, and put it on top of the nearby fifth step. A sudden breeze caught the leather strap and gently moved it, but the bag itself was heavy enough that they didn't have to worry about the wind whipping it over the side. Still, before Rhys could contemplate how they were going to get it, Palomo took a step out onto the fifth stone and picked up the sachet. She turned, stepped back onto solid ground, and handed over the sachet before turning back to the fifth step. She knelt, being careful through yet another gust. "Here. Take my hand."

A stronger gust blustered and pushed the steam from the cavernous area below to level with the land bridge, which obscured everyone's vision. Another blow cleared it, but brought along a volley of lava. Rhys dodged one as it landed near his feet, and looked up just as both Palomo and Lilju cried out in pain.

Palomo brushed at the long sleeve of her uniform, a sizeable hole burned out of it and the olive-complexion skin now bare and blistering red where a handful of lava had landed. He stepped forward and saw Lilju, now a few feet farther down the pillar. The majority of the lava had landed on the librarian's arm, scorching the flesh. Most of the lava had fallen off, though a small, painful amount remained. Tears rolled down her face; the pain had to be agonizing. But she took a couple deep, steadying breaths before trying to pull herself back up.

"Just hold on, Lilju!" Franks called down, then looked across the chasm. "Do you guys have anything that can be used as a rope?" Rhys glanced around at the barren area. "Look for a branch or something."

If there had been anything, it had probably been washed away ages ago. When Rhys focused again on Lilju, his breath caught as she slipped.

With renewed strength, she tightened her grip, then closed her eyes and rested her head against the stone. "Lilji?" she called up. She leaned back and turned her head until she could see where her sister stood, being held back by Captain Franks.

"I'm here, Lilju." Her voice cracked through a sob.

"Lilji, look at me," her sister said. But instead, her sister shook her head and buried herself in the crook of Thomas's shoulder. Thomas put a protective arm around her. "Look at me, sister."

Lilji slowly turned. She held her sleeve like a handkerchief to her face. When she looked at Lilju, she shook her head. "Please hold on. We can get you down."

Lilju turned to look at Rhys and Jason, then back to her sister. "It will be okay." She seemed calm, even as steam poured up from the chasm below, which raised the temperature another twenty degrees. Another small glop of lava fell against her bare leg, and she shook it, slipping further. She looked skyward, then back at her sister. "We have always wanted a real adventure—not just sharing the memories of others. And always remember, I finally had mine." She nodded her head solemnly, then turned to Rhys and Jason. "Thank you," she said quietly.

Another gust, and Lilju slipped a few inches. Jason quietly sobbed at his side.

"Lilji?" she called. "When I close my

eyes, I can see you going on epic adventures with this, your new family. Can you see it?"

Lilji stared, crying.

"Can you see it, Lilji?"

"Not without you," Lilji replied. "You are supposed to be at my side. Always."

"But can you see it, Lilji?" After a beat, Lilju slipped another inch as another gust flushed the area with heat. "Close your eyes. Can you see it?" The wind howled, announcing another breeze. "Can you see it?"

Lilji locked her gaze onto her sister. Her voice was barely above a whisper. "I can see it."

Lilju's voice came as soft as her sister's. "Close your eyes, Lilji." After a beat passed, then a second, Lilju nodded her head.

Lilji nodded back, tucked herself closer to Thomas, and finally closed her eyes tight.

In the chasm, Lilju let go of the pillar and fell into the swimming mass of steam far below.

Chapter Nineteen

While General Landingham deliberated the migration request from someone the world considered the project's largest detractor, he decided he would perform the interview himself.

Everyone who went through the Cludiant had to sit through at least some sort of cursory discussion before they would be allowed farther into the base than the custom auditorium situated near the main gate. It had been specially built for the project and was the closest anyone could get before they were granted permission to step onto Terran soil. And while the interviewing process had become mundane, interviewing Chaske would be anything but. So as soon as the request had officially been logged, Landingham set the appointment for the next morning.

Landingham stood along the far wall of a small office built into the corner of the auditorium as his breakfast of fried eggs and turkey sausage backed up on him. The interview would have been more natural in his own office, where he could have tossed back antacids like they were candy. But because of who he was there for, he was secretly glad to be as far away from the Cludiant as possible. He paced, then turned to the man who sat quietly across the small desk. A man he knew threatened the entire project, but who sat with apparent contentedness across from him. Neither man had spoken a word since he'd taken a seat.

Landingham reached for a cup of coffee that wasn't there, then shook his head. He finally sat down across from one of the only people on two populated planets who got under his skin.

Chaske Oglala.

The fact that Chaske wanted to migrate had come as quite a shock to many. The information had been presented directly to Landingham by a courier who looked like he'd just run two marathons. And for Landingham, the shock of Oglala's request was accompanied by a long stint of heartburn and worry.

He studied Oglala for a second as he sat down and leaned forward on his elbows. "Why?" It was truly the only question that felt appropriate to the situation. He spent several more seconds observing the man he considered his opponent.

Piercing, dark eyes stared back at him.

It seemed like several decades passed before Chaske responded. He pushed a few strands of his long hair behind an ear, then nodded. "Because it is my time," he finally said.

Oglala's voice grated on him. Somehow it always had. But Landingham knew that the project was open to everyone, even if the military wouldn't let certain materials cross the event horizon without being in official military possession the entire time, then surrendered to the owner once they were on Terra and well away from the Cludiant. And maybe even people like Oglala sometimes had a change of heart. But still, his opponent's apparent change of heart painted his thoughts dark. So many unknowns threatened the project.

Landingham considered Oglala's words carefully and started to formulate a question in his head. But for the benefit of the other people who were surely watching—the interviews were all recorded and viewed by those independent of the project to ensure respect and impartiality—he chose his words carefully. "If it is your time, does that mean that your mission on Earth is completed?" He paused, considered his thoughts, and took a deep breath. "Or are you handing the baton off to others?"

Instead of immediately answering him, Chaske gave him a slow blink. When he finally answered, his voice was quiet and deliberate. "If you are referring to Miss Emily Bradley," he started, "she has her own organization and philosophy to consider. And I do not doubt that she will continue the work she deems appropriate."

"You and Miss Bradley are two of the most vocal opponents of the Migration project," Landingham replied. "And I know that, even within your own communities, support for this project remains quite high."

Chaske leaned forward. "In her heart of hearts, Emily Bradley supports people being able to migrate to Terra. But her duty is to the organization she works for, so even though support in the Evangelical community is at eighty percent, she has chosen to be the face of her organization. As such, she deserves a say in our discourse. Just like it is my duty, as well as my right, to protect the planet of my birth. The planet that has given me and my ancestors life. Even as support for the project in my community is almost as high as Miss Bradley's."

"So how can you consider migrating now? Do you consider your job complete?"

Again, Chaske sat quietly across from him for a moment. "Protecting Earth is a full-time job. A job for which every single person needs to be responsible. But have you considered what is going on halfway across the universe on Terra?"

The question caught the general off

guard. "What do you mean?"

"The industrial revolution hastened a great many things on this planet, most of them good. But increased dependence on fossil fuels has given rise to the spread of disease, like black lung for coal miners. Oil has not just sullied our shores, but has wiped out entire species when it has flowed from busted pipelines and cracked hulls. And nuclear energy has left parts of coastlines uninhabitable."

"Exactly," Landingham responded. "So why leave now, before your job here on Earth is complete?"

Chaske smiled. "Maybe you should consider that we have a brand-new planet's future to plan. And maybe the planet needs someone like me to protect her. Keep her shores clean, her mountains intact." He leaned forward, resting his meaty hands on the desk. "Maybe I can do more there than here."

The answer came as a bit of a shock to Landingham, and maybe Chaske was right. But that still didn't cure the feeling of unease that had taken root in his chest since the request came through.

"You know that the scientific team has a mission to remain one-hundred percent renewable on Terra, yes? Each dwelling has already been fitted with solar panels and batteries that more than support their energy requirements. And we have already started transporting materials to build several large wind turbines. Hell, we may even have enough energy that they can start exporting their excess back to Earth."

And there was that uneasy smile again. "Solar panels require the mining of rare minerals. And batteries can store energy, but once they no longer hold a charge, their disposal can irreparably harm the environment." He leaned back in his chair. "You need people there to not only provide for the energy needs of today, but the production and disposal of your energy waste in the future."

It was several seconds before either of them spoke. General Landingham got up and paced a few steps, then turned to Chaske. "You can leave tomorrow at the noon connection. But understand this," he said as he took a seat halfway on the side of the desk, "I will be watching you. Everyone will be watching you."

"I know," was all Chaske said before he broke eye contact. After a beat, he asked, "Is that all?"

Landingham considered him for a moment, then nodded. Chaske nodded in return and walked out as Landingham got up and stepped in front of the camera lens. With a glance back to make sure he was alone, Landingham sighed. "I've got a bad feeling about this one."

⁑

Once Landingham had concluded his business in the interview center, he made his way back to his office, barking commands along the way. The entire situation left him feeling uneasy, and the only way he could work off some of the excess energy was to round up his subordinates on the project and bark orders at them.

Meanwhile, talk of Oglala's migration had been leaked to the press—probably by Oglala himself. What was typically one or two press representatives a week had suddenly turned into two dozen reporters, each armed with a recorder, a pad and paper, and in some cases, a camera and a sound technician. This kind of outburst was a regular thing back when the project was brand new. But now it just served as a distraction. He tried not to show them any contempt, even as his headache grew in intensity. The press area was just off Landingham's office, which gave them the perfect spot for pictures and video of the Cludiant in action. But it also gave the press easy access to him. And as the reporters crowded for photos of Landingham in his office, he took a deep breath and decided to make a statement.

At the last second, he diverted to his

office. He picked up his phone and was put through to the security office for the project. He ordered a meeting to be scheduled within an hour. The voice on the other end of the line vowed to have all security department heads in attendance. "Good," he said, then hung up. And with a swipe at the anger he knew covered his face, he forced a smile, then got up and went to talk to the reporters.

The impromptu status update went about as well as he would have expected; the status of any single person requesting migration status would be kept confidential by the government, so Landingham could not comment one way or the other. But that didn't stop the questions from coming, even as he walked away from the press conference after thirty, soul-achingly slow minutes. He didn't feel any comfort until he was back at a conference room an hour later, a dozen officers and two dozen support staff standing when he entered the room.

As soon as everyone had settled in, he gave an update as to Oglala's request to migrate.

"I don't know what he's playing at," Landingham said, "but we have to be even more vigilant. Especially from the moment he enters the warehouse until he walks onto Terran soil." He looked around the circular table. "Questions? Thoughts?"

After much discussion, it was decided that Chaske Oglala would be allowed to line up with whomever he wanted. However, the line would stop and wait to clear, then Chaske would be sent through the Cludiant by himself, and the line wouldn't resume until he was far clear of the Cludiant on the Terran side. That seemed to assuage fears over anything he might be planning while providing him with his requested migration.

Hopefully Oglala's migration would be uneventful. That may have just been an idle wish, but Landingham had to hold onto something, lest he let his mind wander to too dark a place. And ever since the first request came through, that was where his mind continued to stay. Only time would give him answers to the questions he dared not ask.

When the meeting was dismissed, Landingham answered a few questions once people had filtered out of the room. He glanced up at the clock, noting the time. Twenty-two more hours and he would have his answer.

Chapter Twenty

Chaske Oglala walked out of the interview with General John Landingham with the barest hint of a smile on his face. He walked the short distance to the gate of the base, where a queue of taxies waited. He got into one of the waiting cabs and told the driver to drop him off in the area near his apartment. "Take your time," he said, looking out the back as he waited to see if he was followed.

Turned out, he wasn't.

Not that he trusted the military. And it wasn't like General Landingham didn't hold a great deal of contempt over Chaske's bid to defend Earth. So as soon as they were close enough, Chaske said, "This'll do," and had the cab driver pull them over. He got out of the cab, handed him a crisp $50 bill that more than covered his fare, and began to wander down the street.

Outside an electronics store, Chaske pulled a pre-paid cellphone off an outside display rack. He walked up to the clerk and handed over a few bills, then tossed the receipt into a nearby recycling container.

He opened the texting app and pulled up a phone number from memory. *It's done. 12Noon tomorrow,* was all he texted, then dropped the phone into a pocket. He walked down the busy street and along pavement that stretched too far. Every other store offered disposable items that everyone wanted, but nobody needed. He ached to feel the soil beneath his bare feet. "Soon," he said.

He rounded a corner and looked up; his apartment building loomed in the distance. A chirp caught his attention, so he pulled the phone out of his pocket and clicked the red indicator on the texting app.

Personnel notified.

Plan is now in motion.

Tracking device to be ingested before going to base tomorrow so we know how to time the project.

Good luck.

Chaske smiled as he read and re-read the texts. *Understood. Out,* was all he texted back. He took the back off the phone and removed the battery, then tossed it into a trash bin. He used a knife to pry open the SIM card slot, then slipped the SIM into a pocket. He'd flush it later, maybe after a special meal to celebrate his last night on Earth. As Chaske passed a couple homeless people pushing shopping carts, he carefully dropped the phone itself into one of the carts as he distracted the duo with crisp $100 bills.

Chapter Twenty-One

Lilji was inconsolable at the loss of her sister. Hell, the entire team had been through an emotional rollercoaster right along with her. Rhys, who sometimes had trouble expressing his feelings with words, told Jason that he felt like he'd been "whacked repeatedly with a baseball bat."

The loss of Lilju weighed heavy on them all, especially Captain Franks. Later that afternoon, after they had gotten everyone safely across, sheltered, and Thomas and Palomo had gone out to scare up what little game there was to cook, Franks pulled Rhys and Jason aside to check up on them. But while Rhys felt as well as he could, he was worried about Franks; Lilju's death was the first time that Franks has lost someone for whom she held ultimate responsibility. Everyone knew going in that this process of exploring the universe would be dangerous. But it wasn't until Lilju's death weighed heavy on their hearts that they each truly understood what that responsibility felt like.

By the time Rhys and Jason got back from their own scavenging to the long-neglected yard of the small home they'd taken shelter in, the rain had let up. It remained overcast, with heavy, dark clouds that threatened to let loose at any moment, but for the moment the storm was one thing they didn't have to worry about. Luu, after attending to Lilji and the two scientists, had opened up a courtyard area in the middle of the house, where he was able to start something just slightly smaller than a bonfire. "Went a little overboard," he said as the fire roared between the buildings. "But at least it'll give people a chance to get dry. Maybe stay warm, if this planet gets cold at night."

"It doesn't, Hien." Lilji's pronunciation of the airman's name was nearly perfect. It took a second for Rhys to comprehend what was going on. Instead of hearing her native tongue and having it translate in his head, Rhys heard her speaking English in easy—though clipped—tones. "This planet area doesn't get much cooler than this during evening hours."

Rhys walked up to Lilji and cautiously put a hand on her elbow. "So you're speaking English?" That was what he said aloud, but he knew the expression on his face conveyed worry about how she was holding up. No one could understand what it was to lose a loved one so violently, though Lilji seemed to be doing better than he'd expected.

Lilji gave him a slow blink and a nod, answering his unasked question. "I've been working with your colleagues, Doctors Burnaby and von Schoor," she finally replied. "They've been so very kind in helping me study your language. It is very much a..." She trailed off, looking lost for a second, then nodded. "A jumble right now. I know I will need additional help with your written language, but that will come in time. But I believe I'm verbally passable for now, as you would say."

He smiled at her. "You are." He squeezed her elbow, and got the smallest of smiles from her in return.

The group stood around the fire, transfixed by the flames as they danced over the bundle of kindling Luu had stacked. It was several moments before anyone spoke; the silence gave Rhys time to reflect on the project.

Jason leaned in close and threaded his fingers through Rhys's. "I hope Mom and Dad are okay."

Rhys couldn't help but think about his family, both the one scattered across eastern North America as well as the family he had married into. And then there were his friends, their neighbors. Being two planets away from most everyone he knew and loved did take an emotional toll, even if it wasn't something he'd considered before he and Jason had taken the plunge and moved off-world.

"Hien?" Lilji asked, breaking the silence. "When the fire begins to die down, can you please make a small hot spot for me?" She took the leather sachet from around her neck, closing her eyes and kissing it gently before she turned to the airman. "I should probably start working on this as soon as possible, so I can get you all back to your home."

Franks, who had kept quiet beside Jason, leaned over and put her hand on Lilji's. She brought her other hand up, holding Lilji's hands between her own. "Don't worry about that right now," she said. "There will be time for that later." She turned and faced the fire once again, dropping her hands to her sides. "Besides, this fire isn't going to be of a manageable enough size for you to get close to it any time soon."

As if on cue, heavy footfalls from outside announced Palomo and Thomas's return. They marched into the courtyard, Palomo holding a pair of what looked like Limbo's equivalent of jackrabbits, while Thomas held several large game birds in his hands. "Well, it looks like you two may have just brought us a feast." Franks smiled. "Just need to hunt around for tools to clean these, and then stuff to put them over the fire so we can cook the meat."

Palomo transferred the jackrabbit to her other hand, leaning down to retrieve the scalpel from her boot. "Already on it." She bobbed her head toward the other side of the courtyard. "Think you guys can scare up enough material to create a makeshift spit roast?" Before anyone could answer, she disappeared behind a wall. At least Rhys didn't have to watch the skinning and butchering. He was happily a carnivore—one that appreciated where his food came from but didn't need to know the details.

Franks nodded toward the entranceway Palomo and Thomas had just come through, then looked at Rhys and Jason. "Boys? You wanna help scavenge for some cooking materials?"

"Be happy to." Jason took Rhys's hand into his own, and they disappeared into the late afternoon. There was still a bit of sun lighting the way, which would hopefully be enough for them to find what they needed.

Hours later, with full bellies and enough leftover meat to last them another day, should the need arise, most of the team had fallen asleep. The fire whose flames had once lapped higher than the nearby building's ceiling had shrunk to embers that glowed, casting their makeshift campsite in oranges and reds. Rhys and Franks had stayed awake, Franks insisting that it was up to her to take first watch. But try as he might, Rhys couldn't get comfortable, and so he found meandering conversations much more relaxing.

As Rhys recovered from a bone-cracking yawn, he asked Franks, "How do you do it, Tambra? I mean, we've been awake for what feels like days." But before she could answer, a rustling began near where the others slept. Rhys and Franks watched as Lilji got up and softly stepped around the sleeping members of the team, then settled in next to them. "Did we wake you?" he asked.

"No, no, no," Lilji responded. "I…" She looked away, then wiped an errant tear from her eyes. "Every time I close my eyes, I dream of Lilju." When she turned back to Rhys and

Franks, she had a brave face for the outside world to see, even as Rhys could see her chin quivering in the glow of the embers. She wiped her nose on the singed sleeve of her robes, then pulled the sachet from her neck. "I think there's no better way to honor her memory than to teach you the art of making a charm that can connect two planets." She held one of the blanks and a multi-pronged instrument that looked to Rhys like the metal drawing compass he'd used in high school geometry.

Though Rhys had been sleepy, he was riveted by Lilji's explanation of how the device worked. Lilji explained the entire process from start to finish; the only difficult part was that you had to know the planet's designation. And the only people in the known universe who knew them all were librarians.

"But you can teach us, right?" Rhys held the device between his fingers, twisting the dials as she directed him.

"I believe it is one of the first things I should do upon reaching your home world,"

Lilji replied. "Otherwise, you would have to go back to Comperian."

"What about blanks?" Franks's voice was quiet, like she was intruding on the conversation. "I mean, you only have a certain number of them in that little sachet. Do we have to go back to Comperian for those?"

A demure smile crossed Lilji's face. "The blanks come from another planet." After a pause, she clarified, "Actually, the raw material to make the blanks comes from another planet. It just has to be melted down and molded." She tapped the side of her head. "I have that knowledge as well."

"And that planet?" Rhys asked. "You know which one that is?"

Lilji's smile grew. "You might say that, yes." As she rubbed the blank in her hands with a thumb, she added, "That planet's catalog designation is one."

*
**

It didn't take much time at all for Rhys, under Lilji's supervision, to complete the charm that would connect them back to Terra. For such a complex system of addressing and connecting between planets that spanned the galaxy, the process to make a key connecting them all was surprisingly simple.

Rhys and Lilji left Franks at her post and tried to get a little bit of sleep. As soon as Rhys lay down next to Jason, it took no time at all for Jason to roll over and pull Rhys to him; even asleep on a strange planet, Jason seemed to know precisely where Rhys was. And as slumber finally took him, Rhys dreamt of nothing but exploring the universe.

A few hours and several colorful dreams later, Rhys was drifting in and out of consciousness when one of the airmen touched him on the arm. Thomas, who had taken over for Franks sometime in the middle of the night, nodded when Rhys sat up, then woke everyone else as soon as there was enough light to make the journey back to the cave. The mood was as lighthearted as the cheerful banter, which sharply contrasted with the day before. They were finally going home. But the moment they approached the chasm crossing, things didn't just turn quiet. They seemed almost clinical.

They crossed the yawning chasm with barely ten words spoken across the entire team. The hike back up to the mouth of the cave took nearly twice as long as the journey down, Rhys and Jason paying particular attention to Lilji along the way. Rhys peppered her with questions about different cultures, while Jason tried to keep the mood as lighthearted as possible. And wherever there was a particularly rocky or slippery area, each would take a side to make sure she was okay.

Franks and Palomo reached the mouth of the cave first, with the rest of the team coming to a halt in the early morning sun. After stopping to catch their breaths, and after everyone had taken their fill from the canteens, Franks nodded. "Okay, ladies and gents. Let's go home." There was even the slightest smile on her face. She nodded once more, then turned and walked into the cave.

Rhys reached out and took Jason's hand as the rest of the team followed Franks. "Hold on." He turned and took one more look over the vast remains of a civilization long dead, then turned back when Jason squeezed his hand.

"You ready, boo?" Jason asked.

Rhys took a deep breath, trying to shake off the worry that felt like it had attached to him since waking up on Comperian what seemed like days ago. "Ready as I'll ever be." He took advantage of their quick moment of privacy and leaned over to kiss Jason. And with a squeeze of his husband's hand, they walked together into the darkness.

Chapter Twenty-Two

The clock in John Landingham's office appeared to crawl. The fact that he'd gotten into his office after a fitful night's sleep made the day seem all that much longer. He reached for his cup of coffee—his fifth of the day—and drained it. Part of him wanted to get another cup, if for no other reason than to waste time. Still, if he wanted to sleep that night, he knew he should lay off. Chaske Oglala's upcoming migration made him jittery, even more than the caffeine coursing through his veins. Words ran together on the page, so he couldn't read. His hands were too shaky to write or type, so he couldn't put together reports. And his mind wandered to too many dark places, so he couldn't get any type of detailed briefing if anyone expected him to remember any part of it.

The light shining into his office from the warehouse dimmed, and it was then that

Landingham realized that the connection to Terra had been cut. Powell, one of the Cludiant technicians, had taken the charm after the morning's first migration, walking it to the nearby safe. To support the movement, they kept the connection open for three different six-hour periods daily, which gave any off-world team two hours to head back to Terra while the connection to Earth had been severed.

He glanced up at the clock again; just 10 A.M. local time, which meant two hours before the next connection. Two hours until his headache would migrate to Terra. As a precaution, he'd sent a few more soldiers across on the first migration period, all fully briefed on Oglala's plans with orders to bring Captain Franks up to speed.

He hadn't talked to Franks in a while. "Sergeant," he barked as he walked out to the administrative area near the Cludiant, "have you heard from Captain Franks? Or anyone from the team that went off-world to Abundance?"

The sergeant looked over her report

from the previous shift. "I'm sorry, sir, but no," she replied. "Franks and her team haven't checked in for over forty-eight hours."

Landingham knew there was a chance Franks's team might not be able to check in, depending on what planet they were exploring. The thing was, it didn't matter one whit what he felt; if Franks and her team didn't check in, there wasn't a hell of a lot he could do about it. "Abundance," he said to the technician. "Is that one we have multiple pendants for?"

The sergeant checked something on her computer, then turned back. "Yes, General."

He considered it for a moment. At least there was the possibility of sending a rescue party if the need arose. Still, Franks and her team had some time. "Let me know the minute we hear from them."

"Yes, General."

With precious little to do while he waited, he headed out of the warehouse and to the auditorium, where the line for interviews was almost as long as the line to migrate. It took him a fair amount of time, but that—as well as nervous energy—he had in abundance.

Landingham walked back into the warehouse just before the stroke of noon. He started for his office, but decided to stand back and watch as the connection between Earth and Terra stabilized. As Powell stood up, the image of an early morning sunrise on Terra came into view, the first of two suns just rising along the horizon. It was a beautiful planet, though Landingham hadn't had a chance to spend much time on it. Yet. That would change, hopefully shortly, as long as Ingrid would continue to put up with him.

With the connection to Terra made, the large doorway to the warehouse opened, bringing with it the noontime sun of the warm Sacramento afternoon. And following closely behind were the sounds of footsteps and livestock. Technicians checked people as they approached, and soon the flow of migrants was underway.

Except for Oglala. He was nowhere to

be seen.

"Sergeant," Landingham called after the first dozen people had crossed between the planets, "where is Chaske Oglala?" Landingham looked up and down the line, but saw no sign of him. "He was supposed to go across as one of the first migrants this afternoon."

Before the sergeant could respond, the sound of a Jeep grew louder. Landingham watched as the Jeep continued past the massive warehouse doors and came to a stop a few feet away. An officer sat in the driver's seat, but it was the person in the passenger seat who caught Landingham's eye.

Chaske Oglala wrapped a meaty hand around the roll bar and got to his feet. "General," he said as he wiped his hands, then held one out to shake.

"Mister Oglala." Landingham took the offered hand.

The migration continued, with people pouring across the event horizon and mostly ignoring the warehouse spectacle. "So that's it,"

Oglala said when he finally turned to gaze at the Cludiant. "Beautiful sunrise, not yet spoiled by airplanes and high rises." He looked back at Landingham with a smirk. As he hiked a thumb up to indicate somewhere behind him, he added, "I was waiting to go with some friends of mine, but your lieutenant here impressed upon me how important it was to you that I go early." He didn't hide the contempt in his expression, or his voice.

"Yes, well"—Landingham gestured to the Cludiant—"the sun is just rising on Terra. You'll have about twenty hours of sunshine to make a day of it."

Oglala nodded, then turned back to the Jeep. He grabbed a couple large duffel bags, swinging one over each shoulder. In a way, Landingham was almost relieved, as well as surprised. He wasn't quite sure that Oglala would actually go through with it. But at least the bags meant he was nearly ready to depart Earth and no longer be a source of heartburn. Still, Landingham had people on Terra whose sole job was to monitor Oglala post-migration. Whatever game Oglala was playing—if he was playing a game at all—wasn't going to harm the project. Not if Landingham had a say about it.

"General," Oglala said, then nodded. He went and joined the line of people waiting for their turn to transit. The line seemed to slow to a crawl, but that was also due to the horse-drawn carriage crossing the event horizon. Horses seemed to spook more than any other animal, so there was usually someone from that group who went on foot, leading the horses across. But for whatever reason, that didn't happen.

It was slightly alarming when Oglala got out of line and jogged up to the front of the carriage where the spooked horses still stood. Landingham watched as two of the MPs carefully pulled out their weapons. "Let me help," Oglala said to the older man who held the reins. The older man—Amish, if his beard and simple attire were any indication—nodded and leaned down, handing the lead over to Chaske. In return, Chaske passed him his duffel bags, the older man handling them with ease. "Thanks." He went to stand in front of the horses, where he leaned in close to them.

Whatever he was doing—it appeared he was talking quietly to the two old mares—wasn't threatening, so Landingham gestured for the two MPs to stand down. "Hut hut!" Oglala called, leading the horses up the first part of the ramp as he walked backward onto Terra. He took his time guiding the horses across the event horizon, stretching out across to the new planet. Landingham watched as the final bit of the carriage stopped glowing blue, now entirely on Terran soil.

A few seconds later Oglala appeared once again, and the older man made a gesture, as if inviting him onto the carriage. But Oglala shook his head and instead took his duffels. And with a final look back at Earth, he turned and walked into the morning sunrise of Terra.

As Oglala's form grew smaller, General Landingham finally let go of a breath he hadn't realized he'd been holding. The worry he'd been carrying for the last couple days had finally fallen away, and he actually managed to feel lighter. He dismissed the officer, who turned the Jeep around, and nodded to the sergeant he'd been talking to before. He smiled. "Well, at least that's done."

"Yes, General."

He started back to his office to assume his usual roost and watch as brave men and women set their sights on an entirely new world to put down roots. Once he got to his door, he turned, hand on the doorframe, just as another carriage lined up to cross over to Terra. "At least now I can—"

A deafening boom rumbled throughout the building, strong enough to rattle the glass in Landingham's office. "What in the blue blazes…" Whatever it was, it was far enough away that it hadn't caused any issue with the Cludiant itself. He got to the doorway in time to see billowing black smoke from the direction of the fuel depot. Everyone seemed to come to a stop and turn, though all anyone could see was the thick, black smoke rising from the other side of the base. He was soon surrounded by others, including several members of the Cludiant team.

Sirens started within seconds, and he knew that whatever the issue was, it would soon be taken care of. But not knowing gave him that much more reason to worry. Landingham decided to stop the migration until they knew what they were dealing with, and turned back to face the Cludiant. He opened his mouth to bark the orders, but before he could, half a dozen people jumped out of the back of the covered wagon. He watched in awe as the two armed MPs were quickly overpowered, stripped of their weapons, and rendered unconscious. "Cut the connection!" he yelled as pandemonium reigned around him.

An insurgent easily subdued Sergeant Powell with a blow to the head, her cap falling to the ground and her usually neat bun falling away. Her hair covered half her face as she crumpled.

From the entryway came another blast,

this time much closer. Several of the military personnel who had been streaming into the warehouse were sent into the air as even more insurgents joined in the fight.

Landingham didn't have a weapon, but knew there was one in his office, so he took advantage of the chaos as the spooked horses dragged the carriage, the back wheels now broken, around the warehouse floor and out into the open. Landingham managed to get to his office and lock the door behind him, pushing his desk in the way to at least slow the insurgents down. He picked up the phone, the connection immediate on the other end, and barked, "Cludiant project threat alpha!" into it, then tossed the receiver as he picked opened the cabinet holding his sidearm.

A pounding started at the door. Past the panoramic window, two men were trying to push past the barrier and get into his office. But a second later, his attention was distracted. He watched as one insurgent ran the length of the Cludiant, a metal pole the size of a broomstick dragging along the floor. It flipped the ramps out of place, leaving the bottom of the Cludiant without barriers. Landingham's blood ran cold as he realized the implications. He took his gun and aimed it through the giant glass pane and shot one of the two men trying to enter. And as the first one dropped, the second one took advantage of the new opening and tried to jump through. Landingham felled him with another shot.

By the time he was finally out of the office, he'd missed the person who had reached down and grabbed the charm. The only thing he got to see was the glint of the pendant as the thief pocketed it, then took off through the Cludiant as the beams started their countdown. He aimed his weapon, trying to get off a shot, but there were too many people running around. And though he didn't care about Oglala's people—he knew they were behind the incident, just didn't know how—he did care about hitting his own people. "Keep the connection open!" he yelled.

A second later, new figures approached the Cludiant, but from Terra. He watched in horror as two men lit several sticks of dynamite—explosives that were heavily controlled on Terra and used only for moving boulders and other projects that needed heavy ordnances. They tossed the sticks through, then ran. There must have been half a dozen sticks littering the floor, more than his people could deal with.

"Get out! Everybody ou—"

Several explosions rocked the warehouse. Landingham was thrown back into the door of his office, a piece of heavy cinderblock glancing off his head. He fell to the ground, barely conscious as yet another explosion went off. A deep groan reverberated around the warehouse as the Cludiant came away from its moorings and began to sway. And as the connection to Terra slipped farther away with each count, he watched as the device finally fell away, part of the massive warehouse wall still attached to the back as it landed with a thud against the now pockmarked concrete floor, crushing several people unfortunate enough to be caught underneath.

Blood fell from the stinging gash on his forehead and dripped into his eyes. And in the stillness that finally settled around the room, John Landingham slumped against the doorway and slipped from consciousness.

Chapter Twenty-Three

Walking into the darkness of the cavern felt more like a memory. Rhys and Jason followed the illumination of a couple glowsticks, ducking around rocks that hung low and jutted out at the sides. He was glad he held Jason's hand tight; despite the eerie green light he was able to keep Jason on the path, even after tripping over his own feet. But beyond the security, he felt immeasurably happy to be getting back home after being gone what felt like months. He just hoped things had gone smoother back on Terra and Earth, because he'd had just about enough excitement to last a few lifetimes.

At least no one had pointed a gun at his head, so that counted as a win.

They came to a stop, everyone gathering around the device bathed in green shadows. Only the sounds of their breathing echoed off the walls.

"Palomo?" Franks gestured to the Cludiant. "If you would, please?"

Jason bumped his shoulder, which made Rhys smile. "I know it's still gonna be hot, but I can't wait to get home. See Mom and Dad. Maybe see if Leslie and Scott have been able to migrate." His voice was quiet as a whisper.

Just as the sound of the charm clicking into place and the smell of ozone permeated the small area they stood in, Rhys replied, "You know Leslie. She's probably charmed half the village by now."

The image of Terra flickered into existence for half an instant, the morning sun shining so bright that it blinded everyone. But just as soon as it appeared, it darkened. A slightly tinny mechanical sound echoed throughout the darkness.

"What is it?" Rhys asked. "What's happening?"

"Sometimes new pendants can do that." Lilji moved up to the front and squatted down next to Palomo, holding out a hand. "It connects for a second, but isn't seated just right and cuts out." She took the charm and wiped it on the burned material of her robes.

"Are we going to have to go recreate it?" Franks asked.

"No, no, no." Lilji leaned down and gingerly slotted the charm into place again. Except this time she used more force when seating it into place, and almost instantly, the image of Terra came into view a second time. "Sometimes you just have to push it a little... Captain?"

All eyes settled on the landscape of Terra. The Cludiant was kept in an area a few dozen yards from the camp, and unless it was during migration, the area was generally free of people. Only now the small clearing was full of military personnel, all of them armed, most of the weapons trained on them. And in the distance, dark smoke billowed.

Jason dropped Rhys's hand. "What the hell?"

In an instant, Franks went from the

easygoing leader they'd been with the last two days to a disciplined, no-nonsense commander. "Report!" she barked as they crossed the event horizon. Rhys was hit with a wall of heat as soon as he stepped onto Terran soil, but it was the smoke billowing in the distance and the airmen who looked as if they were on edge that he noticed. "What's going on, Airman?"

"There's been an attack, ma'am," Airman Green announced.

"What kind of attack, Marcel?" Franks asked. She patted her sides as if grabbing for her gun, then turned to Palomo, Thomas, and Luu and gave them a command. "Weapons."

The trio of airmen double-timed it toward the barracks. And even though none of them had rested all that well during the entire off-world trip, even Rhys was fired up enough to help battle whatever had attacked them.

"Not us, Captain," Green said. "It was Earth."

Rhys's blood ran cold as memories of the attack he and Jason had suffered ran through his memories. If there was an attack on the base where the Cludiant was stored, they could be stuck on Terra for the rest of their lives. And while they had access to the rest of the universe, was it possible they were cut off from their homeworld?

Airman Green went on to describe what had happened. "I wasn't here, ma'am, but others were nearby. Apparently there were a few people who had stolen some munitions that we just found about. From what we can tell, some sort of fight broke out in the warehouse where the Cludiant is stored. At least two people on Terra approached the Cludiant during the scuffle and threw in a few sticks of dynamite, though it appears at least one of the sticks was thrown back onto Terran soil, which caused the fire back there. The connection between here and Earth went out, and they haven't tried to connect with us again."

"How long ago was this?" Franks asked as the three airmen approached. She reached out and took the handgun Airman Palomo handed her.

"No more than five minutes ago, Captain."

She considered it a moment. "What about the two who threw the explosives?"

Green shook his head. "Sorry, ma'am. We're going off of what we heard from one of the migrators from Earth." He looked at the other soldiers, all of them shaking their heads.

Franks nodded. "Green? Split your team in half. Half of them stay here and guard the Cludiant until further notice. The other half head back and gather as many airmen as you can from their quarters. Find out what the person who saw the dynamite being thrown saw, and then take every single airman you can and search for them." She took a breath, then turned. "Thomas? Palomo? Luu? You're with me." She turned Rhys, Jason, Lilji, and the scientists. "The rest of you either head back to the village to help with the cleanup, check in with your folks, get Lilji set up in a cabin, and whatever else you need."

Burnaby and von Schoor took the shell-shocked Lilji by the elbow and started leading her toward the village, but Rhys and Jason didn't budge. "Tam?" Jason said. "We're staying here." He chanced a glance at Rhys, who nodded.

"Whatever we can do to help." In a way, Rhys found himself surprised by his declaration. But Tambra Franks was like family, and just as cut off from Earth—and probably feeling just as helpless—as them.

Franks nodded, then turned to Palomo. She held out her hand to Jason and made a small *hand it over* motion. "So we don't have to get the backup out of storage." Jason paused a moment, so she added, "I'll give it back when we're done. Promise."

"Sorry, sorry," Jason replied. "Of course." He took the chain from around his neck and undid the clasp, letting the charm fall into Franks's open palm.

Franks knelt to get to the open slot on the Cludiant. She put the pendant right above it, then turned. "Weapons at the ready," she ordered. "No telling what we're going to find." Rhys found himself taking a deep breath as Franks dropped the charm into the slot, then clicked it into place.

The quick smell of ozone wafted through the air, but instead of seeing the warehouse, all Rhys could see was what looked like pockmarked concrete with bits of wood and spatters of blood spread across the darkened surface.

"Oh my god," Palomo said. "Look." She pointed to the lower corner of the Cludiant, where there was a mass of red. But this time it wasn't blood. The lower right-hand side of the Cludiant back on Earth was resting on a person's head, the mouth open and blood dripping from dead, unseeing eyes.

"Sergeant Powell," Franks said quietly. As soon as the name had been uttered, it reminded Rhys instantly of the tireless sergeant who always had a smile for him and Jason as they traversed between planets. Out of the corner of his eye, he spotted Luu cross himself.

"Damn whoever did this." Franks turned. "We need to get the Cludiant raised so we can get through. Render aid, if needed."

He watched airmen Thomas and Luu have a conversation with the smallest of expressions. "We got this, ma'am." Thomas pushed to the front and knelt in front of the Cludiant. Rhys figured they could scoot under if they went through on their backs, and then they would be able to stand up on the other side and raise the Cludiant. Hopefully enough wall remained to lean it against. If not, they would have to figure something out.

"Wait, wait," Franks said. "I should go first to assess the situation."

"With all due respect, ma'am," Luu replied, "you're the highest-ranking officer on this planet. Honestly, we can't afford to lose you right now."

Franks visibly shook for a second, then sighed.

"Especially since we don't know what's on the other side, Captain," Thomas said.

After another few seconds, Franks nodded, then gestured for the Cludiant. "Okay, but you guys come right back if something is screwed up. We can wait it out if insurgents took over the base." She sighed, then knelt. "I'll be ready to pull the connection if we need to."

"Yes, ma'am," Thomas and Luu replied in unison. They leaned down, got onto their backs, and inched toward the Cludiant. It looked uncomfortable, especially since they had to lay on the beam on the Terran side, while the beam on Earth was barely an inch off the floor. As they inched forward, their arms and heads glowed blue as they crossed the event horizon. It took what seemed like an hour, but they were finally up to their chests, their legs half a universe away on Terran soil as they tried to make purchase.

The beam raised a few inches, and Luu continued to scoot through the Cludiant, his feet disappearing into the event horizon while Thomas continued to lay on the ground, his feet wiggling. In a dizzying move, the view of the

Cludiant suddenly changed, filling the Cludiant on Terra with a sweeping view as the device was put upright. Luu and another three soldiers came into view, two on each side, before Luu leaned down and pulled Thomas through the Cludiant.

It was then that they finally got a chance to see the destruction on Earth. Whatever happened must have happened quickly, without regard for safety or human life. As he scanned the area, his eyes landed on a lifeless and bloodied figure.

"General Landingham," Rhys said, then ran through the gate.

The end...for now

About The Author

Walter Hopgood is a fifty-something year old heterosexually impaired (yes, gay) guy that lives in Oregon, with his husband of 27+ years, and a dog that doesn't seem to be able to completely sleep through the night. He's been writing for decades, though not professionally until 2016. *Migration: Beginnings* is his first foray into fiction work, whereas he and cowriter Lisa Witte previously published a non-fiction travel book, *A Million Miles Amok: A Guidebook for the New Road Warrior* prior to the start of the Migration series. Walter is an office drone by day, working in the medical I.T. field. A Pharmacy Technician by trade, Walter travels around the country helping hospitals implement electronic medical records (eMAR) software that betters physician workflows, helps with clinical decision making, and above all, keeps patients safe.

When Walter isn't traveling or working, he spends as much time writing as possible. Though he currently has only two books out as of this writing, he has several more planned in the *Migration* series, and a new romance series planned with cowriter Lisa. You can connect with him online.

Email: walter@walterwrites.com
Twitter: @WalterWrites
Website: https://walterwrites.com
Instagram: @WalterWrites

Books by Walter Hopgood

A Million Miles Amok: A Guidebook for The New Road Warrior (with co-author Lisa Witte)
Migration: Beginnings (Migration Series, Book One)
Migration: Knowledge (Migration Series, Book Two)